PRAISE FOR THE DRAMA HIGH SERIES

"You'll definitely feel for Jayd Jackson, the bold sixteen-year-old Compton, California, junior at the center of keep-it-real Drama High stories."

—*Essence* magazine on *Drama High: Jayd's Legacy*

"Edged with comedy and a provoking street-savvy plot line, Compton native and Drama High author L. Divine writes a fascinating story capturing the voice of young black America."

—*The Cincinnati Herald* on the *Drama High Series*

"Filled with all the elements that make for a good book—young love, non-stop drama and a taste of the supernatural, it is sure to please."

—THE RAWSISTAZ Reviewers on *Drama High: The Fight*

". . . A captivating look at teen life."

—Harriet Klausner on *Drama High: The Fight*

"If you grew up on a steady diet of saccharine *Sweet Valley* novels and think there aren't enough books specifically for African American teens, you're in luck."

—*Prince George's Sentinel* on *Drama High: The Fight*

"Through a healthy mix of book smarts, life experiences, and down-to-earth flavor, L. Divine has crafted a well-nuanced coming-of-age tale for African-American youth."

—*The Atlanta Voice* on *Drama High: The Fight*

"*Drama High* has it all . . . fun, fast, addictive."

—Cara Lockwood, bestselling author of *Moby Clique*

Also by L. Divine

THE FIGHT

SECOND CHANCE

JAYD'S LEGACY

FRENEMIES

LADY J

COURTIN' JAYD

HUSTLIN'

Published by Kensington Publishing Corporation

Drama High, Vol. 8
KEEP IT MOVIN'

L. Divine

KENSINGTON PUBLISHING CORP.
www.kensingtonbooks.com

This volume, *Keep It Movin'*, is special to me because the term is more than just slang. It reaches back to our collective ancestors who always kept it moving in spite of the insurmountable odds they faced. It is also dedicated to their descendants, those of us who continue their legacy through dreaming, working, and living. If you are taking breath, be thankful and don't waste any time dwelling on the negative. Our past is more than slavery and our reality bigger and more purposeful than the negativisms all around us.

Rather than focus on nihilistic behavior, those of us who possess the soul of warrior survivors keep it movin' no matter what. It's not easy because the world around us—family, friends, enemies, co-workers, etc.—can really work our nerves! But it's all a part of the challenge, an obstacle on the road to success. But anyone who is self-employed through the blessings of his/her talent will tell you that it's worth all of the DRAMA.

Our ancestors knew it and strived to always do their own work, and when that wasn't possible, they still made a way. We have the opportunity through education, self-love and realization—and most of all, through faith—to surpass their contributions and keep our legacy alive and ever-flowing.

So, this volume is dedicated to the FAITHFUL who prevail against the odds, always tred the path less walked upon, and who not only know their flow but live it. As the saying goes, "don't give up, get up" and keep it movin' always~

*"You can't hide the truth from the youth/
You can steal the fruit not the root."*

—ETANA

ACKNOWLEDGMENTS

To my babies: Without you two, I wouldn't have the vision to do half of what I do every day.

To Kenya, Christine, Deanna, Crystal, and the rest of their family for taking such good care of my babies while I'm on my grind. To my godsister Joliba, who is the quintessential essence of change: You are an inspiration.

To Al, Dawn, and the rest of the folks at Perk Coffeehouse in Glenwood Park for helping me keep my mojo flowing so I can keep on writing.

To all of the single parents raising children with love and sacrifice, mothers in particular: I know it's hard and rough at times, but remember we are raising our future adults. We sacrifice ourselves and yet still find a way to work every day and keep living. You are my she-roes, my role models, my Cinderellas. Thank you, mothers, for your energy.

And to my loyal readers: As long as you keep on reading, I'll keep on writing. Together we keep the series moving forward.

THE CREW

Jayd

A sassy sixteen-year-old from Compton, California, who comes from a long line of Louisiana conjure women. She is the only one in her lineage born with brown eyes and a caul. Her grandmother appropriately named her "Jayd," which is also the name her grandmother took on in her days as a voodoo queen in New Orleans. She lives with her grandparents, four uncles, and her cousin Jay. Jayd is in all AP classes and visits her mother on the weekend. She has a tense relationship with her father, whom she sees occasionally, and has never-ending drama in her life, whether at school or home.

Mama/Lynn Mae

When Jayd gets in over her head, her grandmother, Mama, is always there to help her. A full-time conjure woman with magical green eyes and a long list of both clients and haters, Mama also serves as Jayd's teacher, confidante, and protector.

Mom/Lynn Marie

At thirty-something years old, Lynn Marie would never be mistaken for a mother of a teenager. But Jayd's mom is definitely all that and with her green eyes, she keeps the men guessing. Able to talk to Jayd telepathically, Lynn Marie is always there when Jayd needs her.

Esmeralda

Mama's nemesis and Jayd's nightmare, this next-door neighbor is anything but friendly. She relocated to Compton from Louisiana around the same time Mama did and has been a thorn in Mama's side ever since. She continuously causes trouble for Mama and Jayd. Esmeralda's cold blue eyes have powers of their own, although not nearly as powerful as Mama's.

Rah
Rah is Jayd's first love from junior high school who has come back into her life when a mutual friend, Nigel, transfers from Rah's high school (Westingle) to South Bay. He knows everything about her and is her spiritual confidant. Rah lives in Los Angeles but grew up with his grandparents in Compton like Jayd. He loves Jayd fiercely but has a girlfriend who refuses to go away (Trish) and a baby-mama (Sandy). Rah is a hustler by necessity and a music producer by talent. He takes care of his younger brother Kamal and holds the house down while his dad is locked up and his mother strips at a local club.

Misty
The word "frenemies" was coined for this former best friend of Jayd's. Misty has made it her mission to sabotage Jayd any way she can. Living around the corner from Jayd, she has the unique advantage of being an original hater from the neighborhood and at school.

KJ
He's the most popular basketball player on campus, Jayd's ex-boyfriend, and Misty's current boyfriend. Ever since he and Jayd broke up, he's made it his personal mission to persecute her.

Nellie
One of Jayd's best friends, Nellie is the prissy princess of the crew. She is also dating Chance, even though it's Nigel she's really feeling. Nellie made history at South Bay by becoming the first Black Homecoming princess and has let the crown go to her head.

Mickey

The gangster girl of Jayd's small crew. She and Nellie are best friends but often at odds with each other, mostly because Nellie secretly wishes she could be more like Mickey. A true hood girl, she loves being from Compton, and her man with no name is a true gangster. Mickey and Nigel have quickly become South Bay High's newest couple.

Jeremy

A first for Jayd, Jeremy is her white ex-boyfriend who also happens to be the most popular cat at South Bay. Rich, tall and extremely handsome, Jeremy's witty personality and good conversation keep Jayd on her toes and give Rah a run for his money—literally.

Mickey's Man

Never using his name, Mickey's original boyfriend is a trouble-maker and always hot on Mickey's trail. Always in and out of jail, Mickey's man is notorious in her hood for being a cold-hearted gangster, and loves to be in control. He also has a thing for Jayd, but Jayd can't stand to be anywhere near him.

Nigel

The new quarterback on the block, Nigel is a friend of Jayd's from junior high and also Rah's best friend, making Jayd's world even smaller at South Bay High. Nigel is the star football player and dumped his ex-girlfriend at Westingle (Tasha) to be with his new baby-mama-to-be, Mickey. Jayd is caught up in the mix as a friend to them both, but her loyalty lies with Nigel because she's known him longer and he's always had her back.

Chance

The rich, white hip-hop kid of the crew, Chance is Jayd's drama homie and Nellie's boyfriend, if you let him tell it. He used to have a crush on Jayd and now has turned his attention to Nellie.

Bryan

The youngest of Mama's children and Jayd's favorite uncle, Bryan is a dj by night and works at the local grocery store during the day. He's also an acquaintance of both Rah and KJ from playing ball around the hood. Bryan often gives Jayd helpful advice about her problems with boys and hating girls alike. Out of all of Jayd's uncles, Bryan gives her grandparents the least amount of trouble.

Jay

Jay is more like an older brother to Jayd than her cousin. Like Jayd, he lives with Mama but his mother (Mama's youngest daughter) left him when he was a baby and never returned. He doesn't know his father and attends Compton High. He and Jayd often cook together and help Mama around the house.

Prologue

As I stand here with my cell phone to my ear, listening to Rah's rationale about why he has to leave me stranded with no date, to drive all the way out to Pomona to meet Sandy's crazy ass, I can feel my head getting hot. I now know the heat of a thousand suns. The tears well up behind my tired eyes, but I refuse to let him hear me cry. I haven't even made it into the bathroom yet and I already want to throw my cell in the toilet and flush the bull Rah's feeding me.

"Jayd, did you hear what I just said?" Rah asks, responding to my silence. I put the lid down and take a seat on the toilet, slowly removing my beach attire from my afternoon out with Jeremy. I was in a great mood before Rah came by, bursting my bubble. Now, the last thing I feel like doing is going to a party. I'm not in the mood to celebrate a damned thing unless it has something to do with his ex-girlfriends, Sandy and Trish, disappearing from our lives for good. "I'm sorry about this, baby. I'm going to get there and back as fast as I can."

"It's all good, Rah. No worries." My untruthful words are barely audible to me so I know he didn't hear me. Every time he pulls this shit I tell myself it'll be the last time, just like the last time. When will too much finally be enough?

"If there was another way, I'd do it in a heartbeat." Rah

sighs deeply through the phone and I can feel his frustration. I wish he were stronger in his stance with both Sandy and Trish. Maybe I should have made the Bitter Bwoy Brew I concocted to repel his broads, to work on myself instead. This boy's drama is starting to drain me and I'm tired of being his willing victim. "You believe me, don't you, baby?"

"I believe you think you're doing the right thing and that's all that matters."

"I don't like the sound of that," Rah says while I finish undressing, ready to wash up and get back downstairs. I can feel my mom's impatience and I know she's about to give me a psychic earful if I don't hurry up. She wasn't planning on being my ride this evening and I know she has other plans with her boyfriend, Karl, which means I'm cramping her style.

"Well, what do you expect? You not only threw off my day, you also threw off my mother and Karl's plans as well. But like I said, no worries. You've got to go handle your business and so do I. I'll talk to you later," I say, abruptly ending our phone conversation. I need to get all of my tears out and keep it moving if I'm going to make it through the holidays. Otherwise, I'll be stuck in this love quicksand indefinitely and I can't afford to stop for anyone, Rah included.

~ 1 ~
Keep It Movin'

"Keep on moving/
Don't stop like the hands of time."

—SOUL II SOUL

"*Jayd, hurry up and get down here. We've got to get going if Karl and I are going to make it to Mama's dinner in time enough to leave early. We're going to a party at his brother's house afterwards and I don't want to get there too late.*" Leave it to my mom to have an exit plan for a family dinner. "*I heard that, young lady. What happened with Rah? We already have to take you home unexpectedly and that's going to take up even more of our time to be together.*" Why does my mom have to sweat my mind with her telepathic conversation while I'm rushing to get dressed? She can wait another ten minutes and I'll be downstairs with her and Karl where she'll be able to grill me all the way to Compton.

"He had to go get his little girl," I mutter, still in shock that Rah has left me stranded for yet another holiday. What is it with him and all the other broads in his life? How come they can snap their fingers and Rah comes running, usually leaving me behind in the dust? I'm the one he supposedly loves, but what I want always comes last. What the hell?

"*Well, I don't understand what that has to do with him not coming to Mama's, but whatever. Did you tell him he could bring his daughter? I know Mama would love to see the baby.*"

"Mom, can this wait until I'm out of the bathroom, please? I'm trying to wash my face and I still have to pick out an outfit to wear." I didn't want to cry in front of my mom because she would tease me to no end. She's always viewed shedding tears as a weakness, especially if they're falling over a dude. But I can't hold them in any longer, especially not now that I'm looking in the mirror. I trace the tracks of my tears down my cheeks, washing them away in the gentle lather. I wish I could wash away the pain behind them just as easily.

"I already picked out your attire. You're wearing the red dress hanging in my bathroom doorway. Merry Christmas. The shoes are already by the front door. Now, hurry up and get down here. We've got to keep it moving, Jayd, no matter how tough shit is. Stick it out and come on."

"Mom, I'm coming," I say aloud, even if technically I am the only one in the apartment. How am I supposed to concentrate on being jolly with Christmas spirit when the one I want to be with is going to be with someone else—again? Having to give up spending turkey day with Rah to Trish and her brother was one thing. But, Rah passing up my grandmother's Christmas Eve dinner to meet up with Sandy's trifling ass is more than I can take.

"Jayd, haven't you figured out that the moment you stop taking Rah's mess will be the moment he stops dishing it out? You should know better by now."

"That's exactly what I said to Rah about Sandy and her baby-mama games. She's playing him, and every time Rah participates in her drama, he's letting her get away with it." I quickly rinse the mango-apricot face scrub from my cheeks before filling the sink with warm water to quickly wash up with. I wish I had time to take a shower, but knowing my mom, she'll leave me if I waste any more of her time.

"Well, it's time to start following your own advice. And the sooner the better, because at the rate you're going, Rah's going to be a distant memory if you don't step up your game. I remember Sandy being a train wreck and if that's how she looks in my memory, I can only imagine what she must look like in your rearview."

"You can only imagine; since when?" I ask, washing the salty ocean residue off my body, ready to slip into my new dress and my mom's shoes, but not before I butter up with some of Mama's Egyptian musk body butter. I only wear the good stuff on special occasions and Mama's creations are the best.

"Jayd, I do allow you some privacy, don't I? I don't want to relive your memories, trust me. What I see in your little head is more than enough. Now, get down here. You've got five minutes." I exit the bathroom and eye the full-length fitted dress hanging in my mother's doorway. Damn, she's got great taste. The Chinese-inspired design of the dress makes it that much more stunning and gives it a classic appearance. *"I thought you'd like it. Don't forget to wear panty hose or Mama will flip out on both of us. Make it quick, Jayd."*

"I'll be right down." As usual, the beach air has made my fresh press frizzy, so a slicked-back ponytail will have to do. I'll have to hook my hair up later on tonight, or in the morning if I'm too tired from this evening's festivities. Mama usually has a full evening of activities planned for everyone to participate in. She loves to play games like Taboo and Pictionary to get the entire family involved. Mama also makes us choose teams, especially since she and Daddy, my grandfather, are always the team captains. Any chance she has to beat Daddy at any game, Mama's taking.

"Nah, nah nah nah. Wait till I get my money right," Kanye serenades as Jeremy's ring tone. Damn, I don't have time for

any more drama today and I just left him less than thirty minutes ago. What could he possibly want now?

"Hey, Jeremy. What's up?" I ask, propping the phone up to my ear with my right shoulder while squeezing into my outfit. I've gained some weight between the holidays and won't be slimming back down until after the winter break. I hope my mom doesn't say anything about me stretching my gift out. It seems like she never gains weight, no matter how much she eats.

"What's up is you," he says, his voice as husky as ever. Damn, he sounds so sexy over the phone. "You want to go out tonight? My friends are having a little get-together at the beach and they asked about you." I know that means his surfing buddies, who will undoubtedly be as high as kites and Jeremy will no doubt be flying right along with them.

"Thank you, but no thank you," I say, putting my heels on before heading out the door. I take a quick glance in the mirror, realizing I have on no lip gloss or eye shadow, making me appear plain in this gorgeous dress. I also need something to cover my arms in these short sleeves or else I'm going to freeze my behind off.

"*Grab a jacket and let's get, little Jayd. You can primp in the car,*" my mom says, this time much more impatiently. I grab my mom's shawl from the coat rack, along with my purse, finally ready to leave. It's after five now and I know Mama's waiting on us before serving dinner.

"I promise I'll stay sober," Jeremy says, missing my point completely. "I really enjoyed kicking it with you today and I'm not ready for it to end."

"Jeremy, I already told you I have plans with my family," I say, slamming the door shut behind me as I run down the stairs. I can see my mom's pissed look from all the way across the street. I bet she could kill someone with one of her looks if she tried hard enough.

"Don't play about that, Jayd. Ever," my mom says way too seriously. I wonder what that's all about.

"Well then, invite me to come to dinner at your house for a change. I'll be happy to escort you, that is unless there's already someone else on your arm?" Oh yeah, that'll go over real well, me bringing my white ex-boyfriend to Christmas dinner at Mama's, even if my original date did stand me up.

"Why not? Enjoy yourself, Jayd. And you know Mama loves company on Christmas Eve. This would be the best time to bring Jeremy if you plan on keeping him around, even if I do disapprove of the little white boy. But at least he's cute and treats you well. And if he meets you there, he can take you home and me and Karl can keep moving like we originally planned. So tell him to meet you there and get your ass in this truck now or he'll be picking you up from here, too."

"You know what, Jeremy," I say, swinging the heavy door of the large SUV open before tossing my Lucky bag onto the seat. I always have to pull myself up high into these large vehicles, messing my dress up and causing me to work too hard. I wish Karl had driven his Camry instead of the Expedition today. "Why don't you meet me there and then we can go out, cool?"

"Very," he says before we hang up. I can hear his smile through the phone. As long as Rah has other interests, so will I, even if Rah is the only ex I really want to be with for Christmas. But like Mama says, gifts may not always come in the packaging I want, but I always get what I need. I just hope she understands that when I show up with Jeremy instead of Rah.

"I must be the luckiest man this holiday, with the two prettiest women in all of LA riding in my car," Karl says while I settle into his ride. He pulls off and heads toward the 405 freeway, which will lead us to the 91, the quickest way to

Mama's side of Compton from Inglewood. I'm going to have
to learn all of the routes, since I'll be driving soon. If I get my
hustle on over the break, I'll have more than enough to make
a nice down payment on something small and economical.
With the high gas prices, I know Karl must be regretting buying this ride.

*"That's why he got the Toyota to drive during the week.
The truck is his weekend car,"* my mom says, psychically defending her man. And I don't blame her. My salty mood is no
excuse for me talking about him. Karl's a sweetie, even if he
is twice our size, and he's good to my mom. What more can
a sistah ask for?

"So, young lady, what did you ask Santa for Christmas this
year?" I like that Karl makes small talk with me without much
effort. When I talk to my daddy it's like pulling teeth without
Novocain.

"A car," I say. My phone, now on vibrate, signals a text
from Rah. I'm through crying over his ass.

> Hey baby. I'm sorry about how this day turned out. I'll try
> and make it back and join you as soon as I can. I love you,
> girl. Don't be mad at me for too long and holla at your boy
> when you get a min.

"Well, I think every teenager has the same thing on her
list," Karl continues, taking my mind away from Rah and back
to my list. A loyal boyfriend's also on the list, but I think
that's too much to ask for, even from Santa. "Anything more
affordable?" Is he asking because he's only making small talk
or because he wants to get me a gift? None of my mom's men
have ever bought me anything.

"Cash always works," I say, just in case this is more than an
innocent probe. I can use all the dividends I can get my
hands on.

"That's my girl," my mom says, gently rubbing Karl's hand sitting on the armrest. If I didn't know better, I'd say they've been in love forever. Hard to believe they've only been dating for a couple of months. "No matter what they say, cash is still king in my wallet."

"So, you don't want the gold American Express card I got you with your name on it for Christmas?" Karl looks at my mom's eyes light up like a little girl on Christmas morning.

"Do I have to pay the bill?" My mom's nothing if not practical when it comes to her finances. Unlike other baby-mamas, her baby-daddy doesn't pay all of her bills. Mickey needs to come and spend the day with my mom to get a taste of what it's like being a single mother, for real.

"What kind of gift would that be?" Karl exits the freeway, only a few minutes away from my grandparents' house. Remembering that Jeremy's never been all the way to my grandparents' house before, I send him a quick text with the address. I'm sure he'll MapQuest it if he needs to.

"Well then, hell yeah, I want my card. Give it up," she says, patting him down like the police.

"I'll give it to you when we get to your mother's house. Back up, woman," he says, attempting to gently push my mom back down in her seat, but my mom's relentless in her quest. I hope Mama finds them as amusing as I do.

See you soon, Lady J.

Jeremy's text has all kinds of undertones in it. I know Jeremy wants us to get back together, but I'm not there. I hope he doesn't think his coming to Mama's house is a step in the direction of a relationship. Friends visit Mama too, and I have to make sure he understands that. The last thing I need is more drama with one of my exes.

~ 2 ~
Merry Xmas

"What's love got to do with it?/
What's love but a secondhand emotion?"

—TINA TURNER

When we pull up to Mama's house, cars are parked on lawns, sidewalks, and everywhere else they can fit. It's always like this on Christmas. All of the prodigal children return home to give and receive guilt gifts, as well as get some good food, which I can't wait to indulge in. When it comes to southern cooking, Mama can give Jeremy's mom a run for her money.

"Hey, Lynn," our neighbor across the street, Mr. Baskett, says to my mom through her open tinted window before he sees her six-foot-two man step out of the truck ahead of us. He's had a crush on my mom forever and ain't facing reality no time soon. But Karl's presence might help change that fact of life.

"Hi, Mr. Baskett," my mom says. Karl walks around to the passenger's side and opens both our doors. He's such a gentleman. "This is my boyfriend, Karl. Karl, Mr. Baskett." Mr. Baskett waves from across the street, too lazy or embarrassed to walk over and shake hands. He, his wife, and their four children each weigh at least three hundred pounds. It's rare to see them hanging outside, but it is a holiday.

"Little Lynn," Daddy says from his seat at one of the two card tables set up in the in the driveway as we step out of the large truck, parked behind a car I don't recognize. Maybe it belongs to my uncle Bryan's new girlfriend, who I'm anxious to meet. It's rare for him to change up his look for a broad, so this one must be special.

"Hey, Daddy," my mom says, wrapping her slender, cocoa arms around my grandfather's neck. "I have someone I want you to meet." Karl stands next to my mom, with me close behind. I never get that warm of a greeting because I'm here all the time.

"Well, this must be the young man taking up all of my daughter's time," Daddy says, looking up at a smiling Karl.

"Are y'all matching on purpose?" my uncle Junior asks, making us all chuckle.

"Yes, it's what cute couples do. You should try it sometime," my mom says, shooting an evil look at her younger brother. My mom rarely has anything nice to say to her brothers if she speaks to them at all. The only one she's cool with is Bryan, and even that's a testy relationship.

"I don't want to be a cute man," Junior says, shuffling the deck of cards before dealing.

"It's not so bad, as long as there's a stunning woman by your side who's making you cute," Karl says. I love a man secure in his masculinity. And it doesn't hurt that he's in love with my mom. There's hope for the brothers yet.

"Now that's a whipped nigga," my uncle Tommy says, claiming his hand without looking up. They always have some shit to say.

"Of course he is. Have you seen your sister?" my uncle Bryan says, winking at us both before reaching up to shake Karl's hand. At least one of them has some manners. "What's up, man? I'm Bryan, and don't pay attention to these other fools. They didn't have their meds today."

"It's all good." Karl hugs my mom tight, waiting for the next move. I walk around them both and kiss Daddy on the cheek before smacking Bryan in the back of the head, my usual loveable greeting for my favorite uncle, and I ignore the rest and they return the favor. One person I can't ignore is Misty's trifling ass going inside of Esmeralda's house next door. I guess Misty and her mother are spending the holiday with Esmeralda's evil ass. I didn't know the devil celebrated Christmas. She glares at me from across the yard and walks back across the porch, disappearing in the multitude of crap lining Esmeralda's house. Maybe they'll help her clean that shit up as a gift.

"Bryan, get in here and help me with this food," Mama shouts through the kitchen window. Bryan's the official taster of the household because he'll tell it like it is under any circumstances, no matter who the cook is.

"I'll go with you," I say, leading the way across the front yard and toward the back gate. The rest of my uncles and company are in the back, smoking, drinking, and doing whatever else they do back there. Ever since Esmeralda caused my headache from hell by staring me down one morning before school a few months ago, I avoid going through the front door at all costs.

"Hey, Frankie," I say to one of our neighbors a couple of houses down. He and his white wife usually stay inside, especially on the holidays, when drunken belligerence can come from anywhere and attack the so-called "sell-out" on the block. He's always been cool with me, and he and Daddy are good friends, so I don't get into all of the other madness.

"We're right behind you," my mom says, leading Karl to the back porch and up the steps that lead into the kitchen. Mama's dog, Lexi, lifts her head slightly, giving Karl the eye before she moves away from her customary post across the threshold, allowing us into Mama's kitchen.

The thick aroma of homemade stuffing and sweet potatoes hits me in the face like a brick. I can't even speak I'm so overwhelmed. The room is filled with all of my favorite foods: potato salad, greens, cornbread, a turkey big enough to feed the entire block, fried chicken, rolls, catfish, several kinds of cakes, peach cobbler, and my absolute favorite, cherry pie. Damn, Mama threw down. She must've been cooking for two days straight to put out all of this food.

"Wow," Karl says, voicing my exact sentiments. Even my mom is smiling through her nervousness. Meeting Mama is always the deal-breaker with her boyfriends. And Mama has been waiting to meet him for a minute.

"Well, if it isn't my girls," Mama says, walking over to kiss us both on the cheek. "And this handsome man must be Karl," she says, also reaching up to give him a kiss on the cheek. I'm glad it is Karl, otherwise that would've been embarrassing.

"Hello, Mrs. James. It's nice to finally meet you," he says, blushing at Mama's compliment.

"Well, don't be so formal. Go on in and have a seat. Bryan, come and get this food so I can feed everyone else." Bryan walks in, takes his mini-plate and sits down at the dining room table, ready to tear into the food.

"Here, sample the potato salad," Mama says, passing a small bowlful to Karl before they take a seat at the dining room table.

"The tree looks beautiful," my mom says, knowing Jay and I put it up. We did do a good job this year. Speak of the devil, Jay pokes his head out of his room, waves at us all and goes right back in. Whenever possible, he likes to be alone in the room he shares with Daddy and Bryan, and I don't blame him. It's rare anyone around here actually gets time to him- or herself.

"Is that a new dress, Jayd?" Mama says from her post at the kitchen doorway. She looks so relaxed in her champagne-colored silk dress with house slippers to match. Christmas Eve

is Mama's favorite day of the year, next to Mother's Day,
which is when she shuts down her shop completely and
sucks in the entire day. Mama and Netta usually take a trip
somewhere and get pampered from head to toe. This year
will be no exception to the unwritten rule, I'm sure.

"No, it's my mom's," I say, eyeing my mom and Karl sitting
at the table, feeding each other forkfuls of Jay's infamous
potato salad. We all have our specialties and that's definitely
one of his. My mom is shameless with her affection for her
new beau. But so far so good where Mama's concerned.
Mama's already peeled one of the name labels off of a gift for
one of my uncles and put Karl's name on it instead. Now, let
one of my uncle's girlfriends get a gift meant for my mother
and all hell will break loose between Mama and my mom.

"Oh. It looks so familiar," Mama says. But the look in her
eyes tells me there's more to it than that. What is she thinking about so fiercely?

"Jayd, you not eating?" my uncle Bryan asks, slamming
down the turkey and gravy, stuffing, sweet potatoes, green
beans and chicken on his plate. Mama really outdid herself
this year. "You don't know what you're missing, girl."

"I'm good right now," I say. Truthfully, I had so much junk
to eat at the beach that I'm too stuffed to take another bite of
anything. But I will gladly take home a plate or three to
munch on for the weekend. I'm sure my stepmother will
have a slamming spread tomorrow too, so I'll be set for the
rest of the week with leftovers.

"Lynn Marie, where'd you say you got that dress from?"
Mama asks, not letting go of her lock on my outfit for a second. Something about the way she's staring at me is making
me feel nauseous. Maybe it's my uncles' cigarette smoke
drifting in from where they're seated outside playing cards
and enjoying some of Daddy's homemade eggnog, spiked
with E&J, no doubt. Karl looks like he's enjoying his fair

share as well. I guess my mom's driving for the rest of the evening.

"I got it from a thrift shop on Melrose earlier this week. I was going to wear it for New Year's, but I thought it would fit Jayd perfectly. Merry Christmas, Jayd," my mom says, winking at me and getting away with not really buying me a gift— again. Mama's honey-brown complexion turns pale, and I can't pick up what's wrong. Noticing my concern for her, Mama looks me in the eye and some of the color returns to her cheeks, but not all of it.

"Jayd, you feeling okay, baby?" Mama asks, walking over to where I'm seated on the couch and checking my forehead for a fever. Mama's green eyes have a red tint across them, indicating just how little sleep she's had recently.

"I should be asking you the same thing," I say, allowing her to quietly probe my eyes, looking for anything but the truth. This whole thing with Rah and Sandy has really gotten out of hand, causing more drama in my life that I don't need. And, with Laura, the hater from school, and Nellie, my ex-friend, hot on my and Mickey's trail, I've got all I can handle on my plate as it is.

"Just because your head's not physically hot doesn't mean you're not hurting." Mama takes my hands out of my lap and cups her hands around mine. Before she can speak another sentence, a wave of shock comes over her and a look of surprise takes over her soft expression. Before I can ask her what's wrong, I'm pulled into Mama's world.

"Jayd, don't resist. Whatever you do, just let it flow," Mama says, holding onto my mind with hers. What the hell?

"Mama, where are we?" I ask, communicating as if she's in one of my dreams. I look around the room, which looks almost the same as far as furniture goes. But it's as if they are in a black-and-white movie, watching the show take place from

the catwalk of a theater. I can hear my mom and the rest of the family in the background, talking and laughing. But Mama and I aren't moving at all.

"I'm not sure yet. But it looks like we are somewhere in the past, Jayd. Just be still and watch. That's all we can do until we see what we came here to see."

Facing the hallway from where we are seated on the couch, Mama and I turn our attention to the voices coming from what is now her bedroom. Usually the woman and man's voices shouting in this house come from my grandparents, but it's not Mama and Daddy's arguing we hear.

"Maman," Mama mumbles in our live dream-state. Even if she was only one when her mother died, Mama can still recognize her voice. *"And that's my father."* Mama's eyes travel as the tall, dark man backs out of the bedroom with a knife at his throat. Maman Marie's hand is extended upward, controlling the blade as she slowly makes her way away from him, holding a baby girl on her hip.

"Mama, is that you?" I ask, but Mama's too engrossed in the scene taking place to answer my query.

"I told you, I want out," Maman says to my great-grandfather, who's smiling wickedly at her and the baby on her hip. But Maman's not joking. A trickle of blood drips down her lip and onto her bare shoulder, revealing more bruising from past beatings. *"Get out of my way, Jon Paul, or you'll leave me with no choice but to cut you in front of your daughter."* So that baby is Mama. What a trip.

"Oh please, Marie. You know you're not going anywhere, especially not with my only child. She has more of my blood than yours anyway." Jon Paul takes a step toward them but is stopped in his tracks by Maman's glowing green eyes.

"She's my daughter and she has my gift of sight. You know the lineage is between mothers and daughters. Back up, Jon Paul," Maman says, allowing the sharp blade to cut

the thick skin covering his Adam's apple and causing him to wince at the recognition of his discomfort. I also think Maman's eyes have scared him, too.

"I see that white man has given you more than expensive gifts this year." Jon Paul tosses the fancy Christmas present in his hand to the floor. A diamond necklace and pretty silk red dress fall out of the box, and Mama's eyes follow them as they fall.

"Jayd, the dress," Mama says, looking at me. It's the same dress I'm wearing. Now, ain't this some eerie shit?

"The dress," I repeat, looking down at the red fabric on my body and across the room at the gift lying on the hall floor. Before I can stay swept up in the irony of the situation, my great-grandmother tries to make it to the front door, but not without a struggle.

"Marie, I told you I'd never let you go and I meant it. Are you seriously going to try and leave a perfectly good black man for that little snot-nose, white boy? You have really lost your mind, no?" Maman continues her backward trek to the front door and our eyes continue to follow her. We can see my mom and uncles enjoying their food and having a good time. My cousin Jay is obsessed with the tree we decorated a couple of weeks ago and is taking inventory of the gifts underneath. But Mama and I aren't concerned with the real world as much as we are with the way this impromptu vision of ours will end.

"That white man has been more of a husband to me and a father to Lynn than you will ever be." Maman takes the knife and shoves it deeper into the already visible wound across his throat. Apparently amused at her attempt to hurt him, the wicked smile returns to Jon Paul's face.

"Ah, but that's the problem, Marie. I am your husband and Lynn's father, which means you both belong to me, no matter who else you decided to whore yourself out to." Jon

Paul grabs my great-grandmother's wrist, forcing her to release her hold on the weapon. The baby starts screaming and the smile is wiped clean off of Jon Paul's face upon hearing the loud noise.

"Let go of me," Maman yells, but it's no use. He's got a firm grip on her and doesn't look like he's letting go anytime soon. *"I'm not your property."*

"As long as you live you will be mine," he says, wrestling her and the baby to the ground, causing baby Lynn to fall out of her mother's grasp. She crawls to sit by the Christmas tree in the dining room, which is very similar in size and stature to the one we actually have now.

"Well, then I'd rather die a free woman than remain a prisoner of yours for the rest of my life." Maman's eyes shimmer, causing Jon Paul to look away from her, but he still maintains his grip on her wrist. Noticing how the pretty jade bracelets on her wrist cascade down her slender arm one by one, Jon Paul touches them, causing Maman to shiver. Those are the same bracelets Mama gave me to wear when I needed the extra protection. I hope they help Maman like they helped me.

"Haven't I always said that your wish is my command, Queen Marie?" Jon Paul pulls the bracelets from Maman's wrist, individually tossing them toward baby Lynn, who hasn't stopped wailing a bit. *"Your legacy will live on through your daughter, since you won't learn how to act like a proper wife."*

"I never wanted to be your wife, Jon Paul, or don't you remember?" Jon Paul moves his hands from her wrist to around her throat. The glow in Maman's eyes grows more intense the tighter he squeezes. Not able to stand her eyes, he looks away without letting go.

"No, Maman. Don't," Mama says. Tears begin to fall down

her cheeks as she relives this moment. I begin to cry as well, even if it's my first time witnessing my great-grandmother's tragic fate. Maman Marie stares at her husband intently, never letting go of her gaze as he tightens his grip around her neck. The veins in Jon Paul's skull begin to pulsate so deeply it looks like they're going to pop right out of his head. What is Maman doing to him?

"Marie," Jon Paul grunts, sounding like he's in some serious pain. *"If you want that white man, you can have him in hell!"*

"Not without you there to lead the way first," Maman whispers, almost on her last breath. Baby Lynn watches the tragedy unfold, unable to help her mother, or so I think. Baby Lynn leans over to grab one of the bracelets and her small, green eyes begin to shimmer just like her mother's. Marie, noticing her daughter's gift, doesn't lose the grip that her green gaze has on her husband but begins to repeat her daughter's name aloud. *"Lynn Mae."*

"Shut up," Jon Paul says, trying desperately to squeeze Maman to death, but it doesn't look like it's going to work this time. Just then, the doorbell rings both in our daydream and in real time. *"The white man's gotten bold coming to our home, or has he been here before?"* Jon Paul looks out of the glass windows lining the wooden door, still holding on to his prey. The guest beats on the door, desperately trying to get in. Baby Lynn and Maman continue to stare at Jon Paul and finally he lets go. He opens the door, pulling Maman's lover in before he has a chance to defend himself.

"Marie, are you okay?" her lover asks, but she's too choked up to say much. Baby Lynn crawls to her mother, still terrified from the traumatic scene we all just witnessed.

"Now she is, ain't that right, Marie?" Jon Paul says sourly before going back into the bedroom.

"Let's go," Maman says. But instead of looking at her lover, she looks dead at Mama and me, snapping us out of her world and back into ours.

"Damn," I whisper under my breath. My head is banging and it's not from my tight ponytail. "What the hell was that?"

"It was a psychic message, Jayd. And your sight must be improving quickly if you were pulled in, too." Mama says. Neither of us moves from our spot on the couch, quietly acclimating ourselves back into the Christmas Eve celebration going on around us.

"Did anyone else notice?" I ask Mama.

"I doubt it. We may feel like we've been gone forever when actually we were probably out for only a few seconds. You saw what I saw, so you know who this dress originally belonged to, right?"

"Maman Marie."

"Yes, Jayd. And for some reason it came back to you as a Christmas gift. It's up to you to find out why." Before we can continue, I notice Jeremy's voice coming from outside. That must've been him knocking at the door. He's earlier than I expected, but it's all good. The time was bound to come sooner or later that my white boy would come to dinner.

"Who's that outside talking to Bryan?" Mama asks, looking out of the window behind our heads at the men outside on the porch, smoking and drinking as usual. Jeremy has made himself comfortable already. Maybe I don't have as much to worry about as I thought.

"That's Jeremy. He's picking me up and we're going to hang out after dinner."

"What happened to Rah? I thought he was bringing the baby by."

"He got caught up with Sandy," I say. Just the thought of them together makes my butt itch.

"You know what happened to Maman when she chose to be with her white lover over my daddy, even if my daddy was the crazier of the two. Be careful, Jayd. Ex men can be more jealous than the current ones." And don't I know it. Rah acted crazy when I started braiding another dude's hair. I can only imagine how crazy he would act if I fell in love with another boy, especially Jeremy. He would probably go ballistic on a sistah and I can't have that.

"I know, Mama. I'll be careful," I say, ready to step outside and join my guest. "Would you like to meet my white boy?" I offer Mama my hand on my way up from the couch. We both could use the spiritual and physical support. That vision took a lot out of us both.

"Of course. I think I may have one more bottle of cologne unclaimed under the tree. You could put his name on it," Mama offers. She always has extra generic gifts for anyone who may happen to drop by.

"I think he's good," I say, looping my right arm through Mama's left and escorting her out of the front door.

"There she is," Daddy says, waving his cigar toward Mama and me. The smell of the various types of smoke present is making my already painful headache pound harder.

"Hey Jayd," Jeremy says. He seems to be enjoying himself already. "Your grandfather was just showing me how to play spades." Oh, this should be good.

"This is my grandmother, but everyone calls her Mama. And this is Jeremy," I say, introducing them. Mama eyes Jeremy carefully, taking in the structure of his face and then some.

"It's nice to finally meet you. Jayd speaks very highly of you." Jeremy reaches his hand out and Mama returns his firm handshake.

"I can say the same thing about you, Jeremy. What's your family doing for Christmas?"

"Oh, we're having a huge brunch in the morning; our traditional thing. Then we'll have our evening free to chill with friends and extended family," Jeremy says, looking back at me. I'm not sure which category he thinks I'm in, but I'm staying on the safe side with friendship.

"Well, that sounds very nice. Are you hungry? We're about to serve dinner in a few moments." Mama looks back through the front door toward the kitchen, where Jay's holding it down.

"My wife's one of the best cooks around," Daddy says, making even my uncles look up at him, surprised he's giving Mama a compliment. But none of us says a word, especially not in front of company. The holidays usually bring out the best in my grandparents and I'm glad for it. If Jeremy came by any other day he'd get the real deal.

"As Jayd has mentioned a couple of hundred times. I can't wait," Jeremy says, making both Mama and me blush.

"Okay, and until then, Junior, get up and let the boy get a hand in," Daddy says. My uncle Junior looks at Daddy and then at Jeremy hard before giving up his place at the table. Bryan looks up from his hand at me before dropping his eyes back down and shaking his head disapprovingly. I know I'm going to get a mouthful about this later, hopefully before he tells Rah. All I need is Bryan running his mouth to Rah before I get a chance to tell him. My Christmas will not be very merry if that happens.

"Come on, Jayd. Let's help your cousin finish up in the kitchen," Mama says, pulling me back inside. "Dinner will be served in ten minutes."

"So, what do you think?" I ask when we're safely out of earshot.

"I think you'd better be careful." I shoot Mama a look that makes her eyes soften. I know what she went through as a little girl, but this is different. Rah isn't nearly as crazy as my great-grandfather was.

"*Don't be so sure*," my mom adds. "*You never know how crazy a man can be until he thinks he's losing you*."

"Listen to your mother, Jayd. We've all been down this road before and we're just trying to spare you some pain if we can." Mama looks across the kitchen and out the front door, with Jay's nosy eyes following hers. He rises from his seat at the kitchen table and looks over Mama's shoulder.

"Who's the white boy playing spades?" Jay asks. After placing the rest of the peeled and chopped potatoes in the large pot of boiling water on the stove, he dries his hands on a kitchen towel. I guess Mama had a craving for more mashed potatoes because there's already enough potato salad here to feed an army.

"That's Jeremy," I say, walking over to the sink and washing my hands. The rolls need to be buttered and it'll be the perfect distraction from everyone's opinion about Jeremy. We're not together anymore, but even our friendship is causing tongues to wag.

"And that's Rah," Jay says, practically running out the front door. He loves drama way too much for me. I look at Mama's shimmering emerald eyes as she stirs the steamy pot on the stove, shaking her head from side to side.

"It's already begun," Mama says. I don't know if she's talking to me or some unknown presence in the room, but her tone is frightening.

"Mama, I know Maman and I are dressed alike, but it's not that serious." But I'm not that naïve. I can feel Rah's heat all the way in here. I'd better get out there before the shit really hits the fan. What's Rah even doing here before he picks Rahima up? Out of all of the days for him to pop up, it had to be the one day Jeremy comes by. What the hell?

"Jayd, there are no coincidences in life," she says as if she just read my thoughts while carefully eyeing my dress. I think I should change before going out with Jeremy. I'd change now if it were the right thing to do. "Please be careful. You don't know what a tangled web you're weaving with these boys."

"Mama, I've got this," I say, smiling at her before exiting the kitchen to face my present mess. Rah really can't say much because had he come through like we originally planned none of this would be happening. But no, as usual I'm left in the background to wait and see what he'll do next. Unfortunately for him, I have options other than to wait for his next move.

"I made my books, fool," Bryan yells at everyone else around the table. My uncles are always competitive no matter what game they're playing. Bryan's new girlfriend's perched up against his chair, rubbing his braids gently. I guess she's pleased with my work.

"What's up, Jayd?" Rah says from where he's standing in the driveway. Jeremy looks up from his hand and smiles at me. I don't know if it's because he's got more tricks up his sleeve or because he thinks he's already won this round. I'll figure him out later. Right now I need to calm an angry Rah down before this holiday turns into a tragedy.

"What's up, Rah?" I pass up my uncles and others on the porch and in the driveway, making my way over to Rah, who walks off to stand on the front lawn. My mom eyes me from her seat at the table in the driveway, next to Karl, who's chewing it up with my Uncle Junior. "I thought you were on your way to get Rahima."

"I see that," he says, shifting his focus back to the porch before staring me down. "I came by because I felt bad about bailing on you, but I see you're already over it."

"That's not fair," I say, grabbing his hand to try to **make** him understand where I'm coming from. "You can't get mad at me because you ditched me and I made other plans."

"I can when it's your ex. Next thing I know you'll be braiding that fool's hair."

"You can't be serious," I say, trying not to raise my voice. Luckily Bryan's stereo is drowning out any conversation within ten feet of it. "Wasn't it less than an hour ago that you ditched me for one of your exes?"

"That's different, Jayd. Sandy's got my baby."

"And where does that leave me?" I didn't expect that to slip out, and from the look in Rah's angry eyes, neither did he. My mom and Mama are staring us down, trying to defuse the situation by flooding my head with thoughts. But my head's too hot to listen to reason. Rah's got some nerve starting shit when it's all his fault.

"*I warned you, girl. Men don't see reason when they think they're losing you. Jealousy's something else.*" I know my mom's right, but what do I do now?

"Dinner's ready." As if hearing my request, Mama comes to the rescue.

"This isn't over, Jayd. I'll catch you tomorrow, unless you already have plans I should know about."

"Go get Rahima and cool off. I'll call you tomorrow," I say, watching the rest of the family and guests file into the crowded house, Jeremy included. If my vision of Maman wasn't warning enough, I don't know what else could convince me to tread lightly in between my two worlds. Maman went through it with her man, Mama with Daddy, and my mom with my father. If I don't know anything else, I know not to give my power to a man, and it starts by never letting them in my head to begin with. I may wear my heart on my sleeve, but my crown is mine to hold on to and so is all of the power that comes along with it.

~ 3 ~
Hair

*"Think about it, take some time and put your eyes together/
We can make this thing right because I don't want no other."*

—JANET JACKSON FT. MISSY ELLIOT

"What was that all about earlier?" Jeremy asks as we make our way down the 405 freeway toward the beach. Tonight we're going to Huntington Beach for the Christmas Eve bonfire. It's been a long time since I've been to Orange County to hang out. The last time was when I was at Family Christian with Rah, Nigel, and the rest of our crew, and it wasn't anything like this night's going to be. I don't know any black people who surf, especially not at night. Noticing me messing with my ponytail, Jeremy lets out a slight laugh. "What's wrong with you?"

"My hair's being testy," I say, looking in the passenger's mirror and attempting to slick down my wayward strands, which is more like a big bush at the moment. I knew I should've braided my hair, but I couldn't find a moment to do it. Now it's going to be frizzy from being by the beach all day and night. Oh well. This Christmas I'll just rock the natural look all the way and I'm already knowing it'll be much to my dad's disapproval. He'll just have to live with it because I'll be damned if I stay up to do my hair tonight. It's already after nine, and I know we're in for a long night.

"I think it looks sexy." Jeremy and his blue eyes are trying to get me in trouble tonight and I'm not having it. Rah's already steaming and there's no need in making that pot boil over. But then again, what he doesn't know won't hurt him.

"I like it when your hair's bushy, too," I say, running my fingers through his thick, wavy curls. If I didn't know better, I'd say Jeremy had a little black in his family. Who knows; maybe he does somewhere down the line.

"Okay, so are you going to continue to ignore my question or tell me what that was all about with Rah?" I look at Jeremy carefully eyeing the road and can't help but wonder how far he thinks our friendship can really go. With Rah and me, I know our only limitation is us. But with Jeremy and his family issues, our limitations are more external.

"That was Rah being Rah," I say, trying to avoid the whole truth. Jeremy might be a little hot if I tell him that Rah was my first invite and I accepted his invitation by default. "Besides, what difference does it make? I'm with you right now and that's all that matters." Did I just say that? I sound too much like a pimp. A vision of Maman and Jon Paul pops into my head, reminding me to be cool. I just saw firsthand what kind of trouble big pimping can get a sistah into.

"Whatever, Jayd. Just let me know if I'm stepping on anyone's toes." Jeremy exits the freeway right by a huge mall where there's no parking at all. It's always packed on Christmas Eve. Personally, I like to catch the after-Christmas sales. Usually Nellie, Mickey, and I would hit up the malls and stay until we couldn't take it anymore. But this year it looks like it'll just be Mickey and me. I have missed hanging with Nellie's bougie ass. I hope she comes to her senses one day because I would hate for her to end up on my permanent shit list, like Misty.

"You'll be the first to know," I say, readjusting my mom's wrap across my shoulders. Luckily I still had a few clothes at Mama's and was able to change out of my inherited dress and into my new Juicy Couture velour sweats and matching top. I'm glad I brought my mom's wrap along because it is chilly out here and I'm still in the car. I can only imagine how cold it's going to be by the beach.

"I somehow doubt that seriously," Jeremy says in a bitter tone. "By the way, that was a sweet gift Chance gave you the other day." I know he's not jealous of Chance's Christmas gift from the cast party last weekend. This fool's really tripping. I wonder if hating is a communicable disease because everyone around me seems to be catching it.

"Oh, come on. You're not seriously tripping over a framed program?" But the way that Jeremy's jaw just tightened its clench tells me he is. Damn, dudes are worse than females when they get emotional.

"Chance and I are just friends, you know that."

"Yeah, best friends. He probably gets the entire answer to his questions when he asks." I didn't realize how salty Jeremy was over that. He's starting to sound like Nellie and that's not good. All I need is another friend spazzing out on me over some bull.

"Jeremy, you can either be jealous over Rah or Chance, but not both. What kind of girl do you think I am?"

"The kind that's wanted by a lot of dudes." Jeremy parks his Mustang in one of the various empty spots lining the shore. It's a perfect night to stargaze: clear and crisp. The smell of burning wood trickles up my nostrils and warms my insides, but not the rest of me. Jeremy's last comment gave me the chills. It sounds way too much like something my great-grandfather would've said to Maman Marie. What the hell?

"You're going to have to trust me, Jeremy. That's all I can say to that." He looks down at me, turns off the engine and kisses me softly on the forehead.

"I do trust you. It's the dudes I don't trust."

"I can't believe you just said that." We both open our car

doors and exit the vehicle. The cold night air runs up my body but it's slightly refreshing. He promptly locks the doors and walks around to the passenger's side, following behind me in silence. "Chance is one of your best friends, too. How do you think that makes him look?"

"Like a dude. Shit, Jayd, you act like I don't know how he felt about you. It doesn't take much to rekindle those same feelings." Jeremy speeds up his stride as he passes me, now walking backwards and facing me. He's lucky I think he's adorable; otherwise I would have been on my way back to Inglewood a long time ago.

"Yeah, but it takes two to light that kind of fire, and I already have enough heat in my life as it is." Jeremy turns around with a stern look on his face. We continue our walk toward the water in silence, and I'm glad for it, too. Walking through the deep, soft sand always gives me a workout and I can't talk and pant at the same time.

When we arrive at the bonfire, there are about a dozen white guys in wet suits ready to night-surf. The moon is full tonight, allowing them and the sharks plenty of light. You would never find my black ass out in that water, especially not this late at night or in cold weather.

"What's up?" Jeremy says to his brother, Justin. Justin's girlfriend, Kristi, is here along with the rest of their surfer crew. Everyone's already started smoking and drinking and Kristi has had a bit too much of both, or so it seems.

"Hey, Jayd," Kristi says. "Come sit by me. I'm not going back in the water anytime soon." I forgot she's also an active surfer chick. I admire her athletic streak, but I can't get down like that, even if her man is fine. Justin looks at me and winks, making me blush. Jeremy looks at me as he suits up, rolls his eyes, and picks up his surfboard like it talked about his mama.

"Hey, I see this cheapskate finally got you a necklace," Justin says.

I gently finger the puka shells round my neck. His brother gave his girl the same gift. Jeremy's good with the gifts, even if most are purchased out of guilt. Now that I'm not his girlfriend anymore, it doesn't bother me as much.

"Let's hit the waves, man. I need a break from land," Jeremy says.

"I know how you feel. See you in a few, babe," Justin says, kissing his inebriated girlfriend on the lips before jogging off behind Jeremy. I hope he gets over himself soon. Until then, I'll just sit here and enjoy the fire. From the looks of it, Kristi's going to be no good to talk with. It's already close to ten and I know Jeremy's going to be in the water for a long time. I'll just get lost in the waves from where I'm sitting and drown my thoughts in the sounds of the shore.

I've been in my zone for a while now and lost track of time over an hour ago. Whether it's day or night, the beach can be equally mesmerizing. Interrupting my vibe, my phone vibrates and Rah's name appears on the ID. Damn, I hope he's not going to sweat me about Jeremy again, but I already know that's too much to ask for.

I got one of my girls. Now, I'm waiting for the other one to stop tripping and act right. I love you, Jayd. Merry Christmas.

It's midnight on the dot and he's my first official Christmas greeting. Why does it have to come with drama? Jeremy and the rest of his crazy group have been in the water the entire time, but it looks like they're wrapping it up now.

"Aren't you cold?" I ask Kristi, who's now fully awake and aware.

"Oh, no. I'm used to it," she says, loading her small pipe

for round two of her highness. "Besides, I can't feel the cold through this poncho."

"Yeah, but you're wearing shorts," I say, eyeing her toned and tanned legs. In the face she looks like a troll doll, but in a cute way. I'm not a boy, but even I admit that her body is banging.

"You'll get used to it, too." Will I ever get used to hanging out with a white boy by the beach? I don't think so, especially if my hair continues to be naughty by nature. Me and frizz on the weekends don't work. It's too much work to try to keep up with my hair during the week, and I'll be damned if I'm going to worry about it on the weekends, too. I get up from my spot next to Kristi and walk around the waning fire to the other side where the flames are still big.

"You really are cold, aren't you?" Kristi says.

"Yes, I am." And I'm ready to go. I need all the rest I can get to deal with my daddy and his folks at the Christmas dinner tomorrow. Hearing my mental wish, Jeremy walks toward us, hopefully ready to go.

"Jayd, you should really considering surfing," Jeremy says, holding his surfboard under his right arm while walking in from the water. He looks like he's in a better mood. His blue eyes shimmer in the moonlight, setting off the golden flecks in his dark brown curls. I stand up, indicating that he shouldn't get too comfortable. As soon as he dries off and changes back into his clothes, we need to be out.

"Why do you say that?" He steps closer to where I'm sitting, looking back at the waves like he's already missing the water. These white boys may like to tempt nature but I don't. As Mama says, we Africans have a keen respect for the living powers in nature and for how small we are in comparison. Jeremy looks at my ass unapologetically. I know I look good in my Juicy Couture, but damn.

"Because you have a nice, low center of gravity," he says,

eyeing me up and down while walking around me to hug me from behind. I could get in some serious trouble with this dude and that's the furthest thing on my to-do list.

"Are you saying I have a big ass?" I ask, playfully tapping his arm as he hugs me tighter.

"Yeah. Is that a problem?" Jeremy asks, looking down at me. I roll my eyes at him and can't help but smile. He always has that effect on me. I wish I showed more teeth than tears with Rah. Maybe then we wouldn't have so much drama in our relationship.

"No comment," I say, pulling away from Jeremy. I don't want anyone here thinking I'm his girl again, even if his hugs are next to heaven.

"You guys aren't taking off already, are you? We haven't even passed the bong around yet," Jason says, blowing smoke as he speaks. "You're breaking tradition, dude."

"It's time to start some new traditions," Jeremy says while taking my right hand in his left, ready to leave his brother and the rest of their crew behind for me. How sweet is that? "I'll check you guys tomorrow."

"Later, y'all," I say, waving at the crew and following Jeremy. "You know you didn't have to leave if you weren't ready to," I say, panting as we hike back toward the car. If I keep hanging out by the beach my legs will be as ripped as Venus Williams's.

"I made you a promise, didn't I?" Jeremy slows down, allowing me to catch my breath. I'm ready to get out of the cold night air, but my short legs can only move so fast. Noticing my shivering, Jeremy looks concerned. He steps behind me, encloses me in a bear hug from behind and starts rubbing my arms vigorously, as if we need any more heat between us.

"Jayd, where's your coat? It's damn-near forty degrees out here once you leave the fireside," Jeremy says, stating the obvious. The full moon is directly over our heads, lighting our path. It's a beautiful night but way too chilly for my bones. Mama would be pissed if she knew I was out here without a coat, but what can I do? I only have enough money for the basics, and layering up has always been my way around purchasing a coat that would cost about the same as a complete outfit.

"I don't have one," I say, following Jeremy back to the car. I'm walking so fast it probably looks like a sprint from afar. "Well, not yet. I'm a little behind on my winter shopping this year." Jeremy presses his alarm remote, unlocking the doors, and I let myself into the passenger's side while he puts his wet clothes in the back. His brother took his surfboard in his truck, so he doesn't have to worry about mounting that thing on the roof and can get in and turn the heater on full blast.

"Why didn't your parents buy one for you?" Jeremy just doesn't understand my world.

"Clothing is my responsibility. They handle the basics." Jeremy starts the engine and turns the heat on high.

"I thought clothes were a part of the basics." Jeremy takes his huge North Face jacket out of the backseat and wraps it around my shoulders. Now this feels good and it smells good, too. This heavy thing must have cost at least two bills. I wish I could afford a nice jacket like this, but my car comes first. I'll just have to settle for one of the off-brands I'll hopefully find on sale the day after Christmas.

"Thank you, smart-ass," I say, reluctantly enjoying the doting. But I could use less patronizing from this cat. He gets on my nerves with that shit.

"Jayd, I'm just saying. I met your family tonight and no one looks hungry," he says.

"Looks can be deceiving." Jeremy smiles at me before moving in for the kiss he's been holding back all night and I let him. His kisses are too nice to resist. Before we can get too comfortable with each other's lips, Laura, Reid, and Nellie show up, causing me to feel a twinge of pain. How is it that Nellie can be such a good friend one day and stab me in the back the next?

"Leaving so soon? We're just about to light it up," Reid says, hopping over the side of his mini Benz and letting Nellie out of the barely-there backseat before walking around to open Laura's door. I wonder how Nellie's newfound clique is affecting her relationship with Chance? I know he's sprung, but even he has his pride and his loyalty to Jeremy would never allow him to roll hard with Reid.

"You don't smoke," Laura says, deflating her man's corny line before Jeremy has a chance to respond. Why do the bitches always get a man, not that I envy her little dude at all, but still? I need to step up my bitch game if I'm going to lock down a boyfriend of my own when I'm ready.

"What happened to your hair?" I know Nellie's not talking shit. Her new weave's hanging so far down her back no one would ever believe that mane belongs to her. And it looks hella expensive: must be a Christmas gift from Chance. How much is he shelling out on her?

"Nature. What happened to yours, a horse?" Nellie's eyes narrow in anger and I feel her embarrassment. Sistahs don't usually talk about the secrets of the trade in front of white folks, but she started it and I could care less about her little feelings getting hurt. She didn't care about me when she decided to tell Laura about me signing Mickey's note. When Mickey asked me to do it, I knew it was wrong, but I can't take it back now.

"Shut up, Jayd. You're just jealous," she says, flicking her black tresses over her shoulder, just like Laura does. Oh, this is too much for me to stomach.

"Yeah, that's it. I'm jealous that you're hiding your perfectly healthy hair under some fake shit."

"It's better than looking like Angela Davis without the fist." Jeremy, Reid, and Laura look on as we battle it out. Black history's way out of their league.

"I'm surprised you know who Angela Davis is and I've got your fist," I say, smiling at my former homegirl. Damn, she's on it tonight. It must be the full moon.

"I know a lot of shit, remember that." Nellie's threat isn't veiled at all and it's about time to call her on her shit. I'm tired of playing with her. If she wants to ball with the big girls, now's the time to take it to the court, for real.

"Yeah, the type of shit only a best friend would know, right, Nellie? So, does Laura know all of your secrets too, or are you just divulging me and Mickey's business to the broad?" Both girls look at me, shell-shocked. I guess Chance really did give up the family jewels when he told me about how Nellie has to sell out to hang with Laura.

"Remember, payback's a bitch," Laura says, crossing her skinny arms over her flat chest. If she didn't have money and wasn't dating Reid, she'd be a plain Jane.

"Yes, I can be and I didn't even have to read any books on the subject, unlike the two of you. Go figure." When Tania was here, they had their own book club on how to be a better bitch.

"Just shut up, Jayd," Nellie says. "You don't know what you're talking about." Nellie looks nervously at Laura, who looks pissed that I know one of their hazing requirements. But I'm on a roll and I'm going to keep on going until I get what I want: total humiliation for Laura and her wack-ass crew, even if Nellie's now a part of it. It was her choice to sell her soul to the devil and it's mine to drive them all back to hell where they belong.

"You didn't really think you'd get away with selling us out, now did you, Nellie? You haven't even seen what's in store for you yet, but you will when we get back to campus in a couple of weeks. Have a nice break." Not knowing what else to say or do, she and Laura follow Reid toward the beach so we can finally leave.

"Merry Christmas," Jeremy yells after them sarcastically before pulling off. It's going to be a long drive back to Inglewood, but I'm sure we'll make the best of our time together. He rolls up both of our windows and heads toward the freeway.

"I don't know what's up with Nellie. Have you talked to Chance about her?"

"We don't talk about stuff like that, Jayd. We're not girls. The less I know about his love life, the better."

"Love life? Nellie doesn't have a love life." Portishead's melodic beat slowly creeps through the speakers, mellowing out our vibe. This night would've ended perfectly if I hadn't run into Nellie. What the hell?

"You're kidding. Nellie's a virgin?" Jeremy looks as surprised as I did when I first found out. Nellie carries herself like a grown-ass woman, but underneath her bougie exterior she's really a prude.

"She's not only a member of our club, but she's also the president." Mickey used to tease us all of the time about our status, but I'm proud to be a card-carrying member, and so was Nellie until Tania and Laura came along. Now I don't even recognize my girl.

"Well, that'll change quickly if she keeps hanging out with Laura. Virgins aren't allowed in that clique." I wonder if Nellie knows about this prerequisite? If she were still my friend I'd feel obligated to tell her. But I'm out of it now. She's on her own with this one.

"She's still your friend, Jayd. Nellie's just tripping." My mom doesn't even take holidays off from invading my mind, I see. *"And hurry up and get home. You need to rest before you hook up my hair tomorrow."*

"Mom, I'm not even doing my own hair tomorrow. I'm taking the day off."

"Girl, please. If you want to eat, you'll get those combs out and get to it."

"Fine, Mom. Consider it my gift to you."

"Why, thank you. Now, remember what I said about Nellie. If those girls mean her harm, you have to let her know. If she doesn't listen, make her. Bye." Why is it always my responsibility to do right? Just once I'd like to flip out like Misty or Nellie, damn who it ends up hurting. But I want to eat breakfast so I'll think about taking my mom's advice, for now.

"Everything good?" Jeremy asks, settling into a cruising speed. He rests his right hand on my thigh like he used to when we were dating. I'm tempted to move it, but I don't mind so much.

"Yeah, it's all good. Just thinking about tomorrow."

"Stay in the moment with me for a little longer, if you don't mind." And that's just what I'm going to do. I look at Jeremy's olive skin, his loose curls falling over his chiseled cheekbones, tempting me to kiss him softly all over his face. Jeremy allows me an escape from my world in more ways than one. And tomorrow's going to be a day that can't come slow enough. So I'll enjoy the rest of this moment before it's gone.

It's a tradition for my mom to make me whatever I want to eat for breakfast on Christmas morning. It's the best gift she can give me, especially since—for as long as I can remember—Christmas Day has always belonged to my dad. I requested Belgian waffles this year, but I already know that's not happening because she didn't make it to the store, with all of her holiday partying and whatnot. But from the sounds of her banging away at the dishes in the kitchen, something's going to be made this morning and I'm glad because a sistah's hungry.

After Jeremy dropped me off last night, I came upstairs and fell out on the couch. I didn't hear my mom come in, but I know it was hella late because I didn't get home until well after one in the morning. It makes me wonder if Karl sleeps over when I'm not here. I know they spend most of their time at his apartment, but I'm sure a change of scenery must be nice for the two of them.

"Jayd, heat the skillets, please," my mom says, swishing around the kitchen wearing her old pink robe and a bright flower-patterned scarf tied around her head. She and Karl are spending the day together with his family while I'll be in Compton. Speaking of which, Rah texted me about stopping by with Rahima for a minute before heading over to his grandparents' house, but I'm sure my dad's picking me up early. Maybe we can link up later on while I'm in the area.

"What are we making?" I ask as I intuitively take the two large cast-iron skillets out of the lower cabinet to the right of the stove. Whatever she's making, she'll need these to make it good. Mama gave these skillets to my mother when she got married. It's the only thing my mom took from my daddy's house when she left him. According to both my mom and Mama, cast-iron skillets are the secret to great cooking and healing.

"Banana pancakes with fresh strawberries. I had some when Karl took me to Tahoe for Thanksgiving and have been craving them ever since."

"Cravings? Is someone expecting?" I tease, rubbing my mom's flat belly. From the looks of her body, no one would ever know she's had a baby.

"Hush yourself, child. You know I had my tubes tied after I had you. And after all the hell I raised with Kaiser to get them done back then, I'd better not have any buns cooking in my oven."

"But I've heard of them growing back together, especially with daughters of Oshune. I read one story about it in the spirit book, too." My mom looks unimpressed by my knowledge of the subject and, from her glaring green eyes, I think she's ready to change the topic completely. I must've struck a nerve.

"What was that all about with you and Mama yesterday? I tried to probe your mind but you had some sort of block up. I didn't know you could do that."

"So you did notice," I say, remembering the shared vision back to when Mama was a baby. "I don't know what it was. Mama said my powers are growing if I can see what she sees."

"I thought it was something like that. It felt strange not being able to talk to you mind-to-mind. Don't do that again," she says, pushing me out of the kitchen now that I've done my part.

"I didn't do it on purpose. Don't you think if I could control it, I would?" I walk out of the kitchen, ready to get my day started. I need to shower and get my outfit together for today before I start on my mom's hair. Nellie would be envious of my mother's long, jet-black hair. You can't buy it in any store. Mama says my mom's hair is just like her mother's hair. And, from what I saw yesterday, it is.

"You also need to call Mama before she leaves for the shelter," my mom says, not wasting any time practicing her powers, which only work on me.

"I'm standing right here, Mom."

"I know that. I'm just checking to make sure you didn't figure out a way to keep me out, at least not yet."

"Not yet. And we can call Mama when I get out the shower.

My daddy's supposed to be here at noon, which only leaves me two hours to get everything done."

"Well, get moving because my hair's going to take some time, girl. And I want you to trim my edges too," she says, like it's nothing. Damn, that's going to take another twenty minutes on top of the hour it'll take just to get all of that hair pressed and flat-ironed. "You can eat while you work, girl." What a Christmas this is turning out to be.

After downing my breakfast and hooking my mom's hair up, we called Mama and now I have less than five minutes to get dressed before my dad gets here. I don't have time to iron, and my clothing choices are severely limited. I knew I should've brought all of my clothes with me while I'm at my mom's. One day I'll live in one house, with my own room and dresser drawers to match, I pray. Before I can decide between the less wrinkled of my two outfits lying across the couch, my phone vibrates. My dad doesn't waste any time when he's ready to go.

"Jayd, why aren't you downstairs? You know I hate waiting," my dad says, almost shouting through my small cell. I can't wait to get a better phone, but for now I'm grateful to have my cheap one.

"Sorry. I had to do my mom's hair real quick and it put me behind. I just need to put on my shoes and I'll be right down." I quickly choose the pink-and-white sweat suit and put my pants on two legs at a time. Maybe if I'm real slow he'll leave me behind, but I wouldn't bet on it. My dad likes to show off his children any chance he gets. My brother and sister are grown, so they show up at their own discretion. Too bad I'm still a minor; otherwise my ass would be missing in action more often than not.

"Get a move on it, girl," he says. Through the phone I can hear him open the car door and light a cigarette. I wish he'd stop smoking. "You couldn't do her hair last night?"

"We weren't here." Not that it's any of his business. He's so bossy. I thought Christmas was supposed to be chill. For me, the holiday has always been more drama than it's worth. Speaking of which, Rah's text comes through and I'd rather read it than be grilled unnecessarily by my dad. Rah's still pissed at me for chilling with Jeremy yesterday. Oh well. I can't please everyone and I'm not about to start trying now. "I'll be right down." I'm ready to hang up and check my text, but my dad would rather bitch at me than let me go.

"Hurry up. It's bad enough I had to leave the party at my house to come all the way out here, and I don't want to take too long getting back. Everyone's waiting for us." Just how he likes it, no doubt. We finally end our call and I check my text message real quick before putting on the rest of my clothes.

Merry Christmas again, Jayd. Hope to see you tonight. Call me when you get back to your mom's and hopefully we can all chill. And would you mind hooking a brotha's braids up? You know I got you. Love, Rah.

Anyone reading his texts would say that he was sprung on me, but his sincerity is still questionable in my book. I know he loves me, but not enough to choose me and make me a priority in his life—after Rahima, of course. And when do I get a break from doing hair?

"Never if you're good at your job. Which, apparently, you are," my mom says, answering my question without my actually asking it.

"Mom, you've got to stop doing that," I say to my mom, who's in the kitchen, before checking myself in the mirror one last time before heading out. My puffy ponytail sitting on the top of my head is cute, but I do look like I'm going to another powwow by the beach instead of a family Christmas dinner. Lucky for me I learned a long time ago that it doesn't matter what I show up wearing. The folks on my father's side will always find a reason to hate on a sistah.

"Tell Karl I said Merry Christmas, and y'all have fun." I grab my purse and jacket from the coat rack and check for my daddy's Christmas card in my purse before opening the front door.

"Yeah, you too," my mom says with a sly grin before she spreads herself across the couch: my usual spot. She knows she's pushing it. "See you in the morning, baby." I shut the door and jog down the stairs where my father has parked his car, blocking the long driveway. Why does he have to be so obnoxious?

"Hi, Daddy," I say, giving him a hug and handing him his card. He can't say I never gave him anything. I'm pretty good at making sure everyone gets a card from me for the holidays, but not every year. Sometimes a sistah just can't afford it.

"Hey there, girl. It took you long enough." He looks me up and down and I can feel the speech about my attire coming, but I'm sure he'll wait until we're in the car before he bites into me.

"Yeah, my bad. Perfection takes time." What else am I supposed to say? My mom is flyy and he knows it. And I look pretty cute if I do say so myself, especially considering I didn't have much time to prepare. I'm wearing the yellow rhinestone Bebe sandals Jeremy bought me awhile back, complementing the gold glitter on the sides of my pants and jacket perfectly.

"Tell your mama I said Merry Christmas," my dad says, unlocking the doors to his Infiniti as I walk around to get in. He should give me this car and buy himself another one, but I know that'll never happen.

"She says the same thing," I say, lying to save face.

"What happened to your hair?" My dad looks at my natural do and crinkles up his nose in disapproval. Here we go.

"I came out a black girl, that's what," I say, closing my door and fastening my seatbelt. The sooner we get there, the sooner I can leave.

"Couldn't you fix it up nice? It's Christmas, for God's sake. The whole family will be there." He backs up out of the driveway and heads toward the 105 freeway. I need to pay attention to where we're going from now on since I'll be driving soon. Bus routes are completely different from driving directions, and I can already see my ass getting lost.

"Well, God and I had a little chat and she's cool with the natural me." My dad looks unamused by my reasoning as he speeds down the highway. I love the way this car drives.

"That's blasphemy, Jayd, and on the Lord's birthday, too?"

"Did you check that out with Jesus, because I think he was actually born sometime in the summer." My daddy rolls his eyes at me because I know he knows I learned that in historical Bible class at the school he sent me to. I did a report on the real birth date of Jesus, and the teacher at Family Christian had to give me an A, even if it did debunk their traditional teachings.

"I know you know God ain't no woman," he says, switching to a jazz station to calm his nerves, I assume. He once told me I make his blood pressure rise, just like my mother and grandmother do. I guess it's still true. "What's your grandmother teaching you over there?" If he only knew how loaded that question really is.

"The truth." My little comment silences him for the rest of the ride to Lynwood, and that's the best gift I can get at the moment. I love my daddy, but we rarely see eye-to-eye on anything. If I say the sky is blue he'll say it's purple just to prove me wrong. Mama says it's because we're totally opposite signs, me being an Aries and him a Libra. I'm sure she gave my mother the same warning, since she's the same sign as I am. But, for whatever reason, my mom didn't listen and now we're all stuck with each other. Oh well. If nothing else, dealing with drama in my own family has made my skin thick and it'll have to be extra strong to get through this dinner.

~ 4 ~
Holiday Haters

*"It's alright love/
I let a hater hate."*

—MAINO

When we get to my dad's house, cars are parked everywhere. His block's already tight and there's only parking on one side of the street, so my dad always reserves spaces by stacking cars in his driveway and blocking as many parking spots as he can on the street. The neighbors are hip to my dad's game, but he still gets away with it every year.

"Dad, do you ever consider that your neighbors might want to use some of the parking for their families?" I ask as he pulls up into his driveway, blocking the sidewalk. It looks like the entire cavalry has shown up for the festivities. The smell of turkey, macaroni and cheese, sweet potato pie, and rolls welcomes me out of the car. Whenever my stepmom gets in the kitchen there's sure to be a crowd.

"They can park around the corner. I've been here longer than any of these folks around here and they all know it," he says, taking out a cigarette to smoke before going inside. That's one positive thing I can say about my dad: he could care less what anyone says or thinks about him. I guess I got my "no hater" genes from him, too. Too bad I have to use them to deal with his family as well as the rest of the haters in my life.

As we walk up the driveway and toward the front door I

can see inside where everyone's eating, drinking and talking. This would be fun if I weren't the chosen piñata for the party. I've got my armor on, so they can bring it. I just hope I keep a cool head and don't swing back. Before I can get in the door good the comments start and my ears are already on fire.

"The child's saving grace was her hair, but I see she's let that go too," one of my drunk aunties sitting on the couch whispers loudly to another one, who's more drunk than she is. They've really got their nerve talking shit about me when I can smell the vodka on their tongues from across the room. As much liquor as there is up in this place, if the next-door neighbors light a match this whole house will go up in flames.

"Well, you know she got that from her mother's side," they continue as if I'm not standing right here. I haven't even got all the way in the house yet and they're already hating. How did my mom ever deal with this shit?

"Too bad she didn't get their eyes. Between those green eyes and that chocolate brown skin Lynn Marie's got, she had our little brother sprung off her hot ass for years."

"I wonder if she's gained weight."

"I wonder if her mama's still up to no good."

"I wonder if she's found another man yet." My aunties are enjoying a good laugh at my mother's expense. My mom has always resented the fact that the night she and her sister met my daddy and Jay's daddy, my daddy's sisters didn't bother to tell her that he had a pregnant wife and young daughter at home already. And my mom was so desperate to get out of Mama's house and away from Esmeralda's crazy ass that she didn't bother with a background check on my dad and his family via the neighborhood. I bet she'll never make that mistake again.

"Would you like for me to call her and you can ask her yourself?" My question throws my aunts off guard, and they actually stop playing cards and look up at me, like I'm the one out of line. Damn, this family's got its nerve and then some.

"Young lady, we know your mama's number." They look at each other and suck their teeth.

"And we also know you don't have to call her if you want to talk to her. Or has she lost her powers and her man, too?" What the hell do they know about my mother and her gifts?

"My mother hasn't lost anything," I say, defending her without telling her business. I'll be damned if they're going to sit up in here and talk about my mother in front of me. I know she'll appreciate that.

"Yes I do, little one. But don't waste any more of your energy on them. Your daddy's folks are notorious ashe stealers. Don't give in to their negativity, Jayd. Wear your crown, girl, and forget about them. They can't harm you or me if you learn to block them out."

"Yes, ma'am," I think back. Mama always tells me the same thing. Ever since I can remember Mama has warned about guarding my ashe—or spiritual energy—from negative people, family included. My uncles—except for Bryan—and I rarely interact for the same reason. It hurts Mama to keep herself at bay from her own sons, but protection is protection, no matter who the person doing you harm is. And most ashe leaches—as Netta calls them—aren't aware of their negative power and that makes it worse.

"Those snooty-ass N'awlins girls," my auntie slurs. "I always knew he should've never married a Creole. We used to hear about your grandmother across the border, and she ain't no better than no one." I walk over to post up in the hallway where I can get a better view of the house, which is decorated to the nines. The tree is much smaller than Mama's but still pretty. There's barely any standing room, so I'll claim this spot for now.

"All good things, I hope," I say, wiping the sarcastic smile right off of her face. I know most of the rumors about my lineage aren't good, but that's not our problem. I admit most of my neighbors from New Orleans are haters, but not Mama. The thing I find most peculiar about New Orleans folks is that they tend not to claim Shreveport as a part of the state of Louisiana, which is where my daddy and his folks grew up hanging out, right next to the Texas/Louisiana border. The majority of the folks on his side of Compton are from Mississippi, and that's about as country as it can get.

"Hi, Jayd," my cousin Nia says. I don't speak to her too much, especially since she tried to get with Rah when we were all in school together. She still attends Family Christian and I'm trying to bury the hatchet, but I have a feeling she'll be the first to dig it up and stab me in the back with it if I put it in the ground too deep.

"Jayd," our little cousin Shelley says, hugging me tight. At least someone's happy to see me.

"Hey, sweetie. How's junior high treating you?" I ask, returning her tight hug. I've always loved my little cousin. I used to play with her like a baby doll whenever I saw her. Now she's almost as big as I am, and pretty, too.

"I love it," she says, still naïve of the looming drama Family Christian holds. I hope she stays immune to it through junior high and high school. But I can't help but wonder what happened to her beautiful hair? Damn, she got messed up.

"You should let me do your hair. It'll work wonders for you, trust me." She looks like she got a bad haircut and everyone's lying to her face saying she looks flyy. I've got to help her out, whether she wants me to or not. I can't let my relative walk around looking like she stuck her finger in an electrical outlet when I can easily hook her up. Besides, it'll give me something else to focus on while I'm here.

"Don't let that girl touch your head," my aunt-in-law Sandra says, walking up behind her daughter and pulling Shelley away from me like I've got the plague. I see she's heard about me and my lineage, too. Noticing my hurt look, she tries to clean up her comment, but I know what she means. "I just mean to say she looks beautiful just like this. My daughter-in-law does all of our heads and she's good at it, too." Well, like the saying goes, denial ain't just a river in Egypt and this sistah's shoulder-deep in it.

"Okay. But, if you change your mind you can find me at Netta's Never Nappy Beauty Salon off Greenleaf Boulevard." My cousin's eyes light up at the mention of the shop.

"You mean the shop with the big, pink neon sign and tall Christmas tree in the window? I've always wanted to see inside of that place." Her mother's jaw tightens and she takes the last word on the subject.

"We're not interested in changing stylists but thank you," Sandra says. I forgot how uptight she can be and I doubt it's just because she's a Jehovah's Witness. She's always quick to remind us every year at Christmas that she's only here because my uncle insists that she come. And like a good wife should, in her opinion, she obeys her husband.

"I got you," I say, taking my phone out of my purse and scrolling through my contacts to locate Rah's number. Too bad my daddy's my ride, because it's already time for me to go. Maybe I can catch the bus to Rah's grandparents' house and he can give me a ride back to Inglewood when he goes home. I'm sure there's drama where he is too, but at least it's not mine and I can play with his little girl.

"Jayd, have you seen your stepmother yet? She's in the kitchen," my daddy says, finally walking in from outside and pointing to where all the good food is. I guess I can wait until after I eat and catch up with my stepmom before skipping out.

I pass up my hating auntie and walk through the dining room where more of my cousins and folks are involved in a game of dominoes. I nod what's up to everyone and they return the gesture without much interest. I continue toward the kitchen where my dad walks in ahead of me to give his wife a kiss on the neck and a smack on the ass. What is it with dudes and grabbing women's behinds? She has more than enough booty for his small hands, but really. That looked like it hurt.

"Hey, girl," my stepmother Faye says, turning around from her station at the sink full of dishes and giving me a big hug. She always smells like honeysuckle and food: two of my favorite scents. "Don't you look cute," she says, touching my afro puff and looking me up and down. She always has nice things to say to me. My daddy rolls his eyes at her compliment and walks out of the kitchen toward the back of the house where my uncles and the rest of the crowd are hanging out.

"Well, thank you. So do you," I say, returning the love. How my dad always gets good women on his side baffles me. He is charming and a hardworking brother, both positive attributes. Maybe it's just me he has a problem with.

"So, how's school? Still straight As, I assume." I gave them both hell when I lived here briefly, but I was always a good student academically. It was the social aspect of school I had a problem with.

"School's good and yes, my grades are cool. We have finals coming up after the break, so I'll let you know how many As I get then."

"Oh, I know you'll do fine, Jayd. You've always earned good grades." That means a lot coming from her. Faye went back to school recently to get a bachelor's degree and is already well on her way to earning her master's. She's the only sistah I know who's doing it big like that and she inspires the hell out of me. And she's almost as good in the kitchen as Mama is, which is no easy crown to wear.

"If I get a four-point-zero grade-point average this semester, you think you can convince my daddy to give me his car?"

Faye looks at me, confused, as she continues washing the dishes. "Your daddy didn't show you your Christmas gift yet?" she asks.

"What gift?" I ask, peeking in the pots on the stove. There's so much food in this kitchen I can't even see the countertops. Faye can throw down. When I lived here I gained about twenty pounds. Most of the weight came from being depressed, but eating constantly didn't help either.

"Look outside." I walk over to the back door and notice a silver Nissan Sentra parked in the garage that looks just like the one I drove for my driving lessons. I know he didn't buy me this bucket after I told him I hated it. What the hell? My daddy signals me to come outside and join him.

"Merry Christmas, baby. I bought the car, now you take care of the rest," my daddy says with half the family behind him gawking.

"I don't know what to say." And it's true, I don't. I feel like crying, I'm so pissed he didn't listen to me. But I also know I should be grateful to have a ride, no matter how much I may hate it.

"How about thank you," my auntie says, puffing on her cigarette. Nia looks at me, envious of the attention I'm getting. The only reason she doesn't have a car is because she doesn't want to learn how to drive for some reason. Nellie's the same way, happy to have people chauffeur her black ass all around town. Not me. I'd rather have my own wheels any day. Well, not these wheels, but they'll have to do for now.

"Here are the keys. Why don't you get in and check it out,"

my father says, passing me the two silver keys and egging me on toward the raggedy vehicle. The hubcaps are missing and so is the radio, just like in my mom's ride. It smells like ass because so many people have sat in it and even though I'm not a mechanic, I know this car needs some serious work. Rah and Nigel could probably handle it, but still. How could he put his baby girl in this godforsaken ride?

"I already know what it looks like. I spent two weeks driving it, remember?" He dangles the keys in front of me, waiting for me to take them. I want to leave him hanging and go back in the kitchen to eat, but if I do I know I'll never hear the end of it.

"Yes, I remember. That's why I thought it would be a good first car for you because you're already used to it. Don't you like it?" Now, I would normally take this opportunity to tell him just what I think but I already know how they feel around here about voicing your true feelings. My aunt Sandy was my secret Santa about ten years ago and bought me the ugliest Cabbage Patch suit I'd ever seen. When she asked me what I thought about the gift, I said I didn't like it and my father put me on punishment for the rest of the weekend. That was also the last year they had a secret Santa drawing in this family, or at least that I know of.

"I love it, Daddy. Thank you," I say, lying to his and everyone else's face. My daddy beams with pride and hugs me tight, like he does when I'm agreeable. I feel like I'm the one giving him the gift. I told him I hated this car and he still bought it. Why doesn't he listen to me? My aunties and the rest of the family are busy giving my daddy props for being such a great father and he's loving it. Am I the only one who sees the problem with this picture?

"*I do, baby,*" my mom says, invading my head right on time. Her voice will keep me calm. "*Girl, your daddy does what he wants to, damn your wishes. Don't you get that by now?"* I know my mom's right, but I refuse to think about that right now. I have to save face in front of his family and I can't hear her say "I told you so" while trying to do it.

"You sure are a good daddy, little brother," my aunt says, shooting me an evil look. "You should be grateful, little girl. Everybody doesn't have a daddy like this one." She sips on her drink and holds herself up on her son's shoulder, trying to hide her drunken state. She's such a hater but I don't care. My feelings are valid, no matter what these folks think. They don't have to risk their lives driving this hideous thing.

"Alright, let's pray and get this dinner going. And hey, I can start drinking early this year because Jayd can drive herself home from now on," he says, making everyone in the room laugh. He's right; I've got keys and wheels. The only person stopping me is me, and that ends right now. Maybe it won't be so bad once I fix it up a little bit. Well, at least I have something to roll in and for that I am grateful.

"You alright, baby?" Faye passes me a stacked plate and a fork. She knows me so well. "You don't look like a teenager who just got her first car for Christmas." She's right. I'm far from happy right now. I'm so pissed I can't even eat and that's saying something.

"Yeah, just tired. I got in late last night and got up early this morning to do my mom's hair." I play with the delicious-looking food on my plate, trying to hold back my tears. I need to go somewhere where I can cry my eyes out.

"Yeah, your daddy told me about your new career. Do you really want to do hair for the rest of your life?" I know she doesn't see the pride in my chosen profession for the time being, because she believes academics are the answer to everything, but this time I can't agree.

"I'm only sixteen and I like doing hair." Now my appetite's completely gone. I can't help but feel attacked on a personal level whenever someone demeans our profession. Doing

hair is in my blood and it's a gift, not a curse like she's making it out to be. Faye's always hated on any job that doesn't
require a college degree. My daddy doesn't have a degree,
but she's working on that, too.

"I know that, but Jayd, you could be tutoring or working
at a library or something other than just doing hair. You have
a sharp head and you should use that to get you through."
That's the one thing about Faye I don't get. She's so smart in
one way but clueless when it comes to our cultural heritage,
and I think my dad loves her for that the most. Rah texts me
right before I'm able to comment back to Faye and it's perfect timing. I don't want to take out my anger on her.

"I'll think about that," I say, placing my plate on the
counter while everyone else files into the kitchen, ready to
get their grub on. I think if I skip out now it won't be so bad.

What's up with you? I'm about to take Rahima back to my
house. Need a ride? Holla back at your boy.

"Yes Jayd, I think you should seriously consider it. There
are plenty of part-time jobs at the college I work at. You
should drop by one day and let me introduce you to some of
my coworkers." Ignoring my stepmother completely, I reply
back to Rah in record time. I need to get out of here before I
say something I truly regret and I'm not trying to hurt anyone's feelings today.

Yes, please come follow me back to my mom's first and
then we can kick it. My dad bought me a car and I doubt it'll
make it back to Inglewood. See y'all soon.

"Okay, we'll make it a date," I say, searching the drawers
for aluminum foil. Faye is the queen of Costco and keeps the

house stocked with anything needed in the kitchen and bath-room.

"Where are you rushing off to?" my daddy asks as Faye hands him his plate and a drink. "I knew I should've waited until after dinner to give you the car." He's right. Maybe I'd still have an appetite. Now I'll have to wait until I vent to eat my dinner. Faye piles a plate full of cake and pie for me to take with me along with a bag full of her famous chocolate-chip cookies. If I could perfect this recipe and her sweet potato pie, I'd be a happy black girl.

"Rah's going to check my car out for me and I need to get back. I have an early workday tomorrow," I say, half telling the truth. I'm supposed to be at the shop tomorrow, but there's no time attached to my commitment. Netta has clients coming as early as seven in the morning, but she knows she won't be seeing me until much later. Me and Mickey's shopping day will have to wait until Sunday be-cause tomorrow I'm all about making my money.

"Rah," Faye says loud enough for everyone to hear, in-cluding Nia, whose high-yellow face has just turned a shade of deep red. I know she's hot that Rah and I have maintained our friendship in spite of her hating-ass tricks. But like the rabbit says, tricks are made for kids, and I'm growing up. I can only hope she's doing the same.

"Yeah, Rah. You know he's good at working on cars. He and Nigel would love a new project." I know they're going to clown my ride, but I'm willing to take that risk if it means they can make it look better and drive safer. When I drove it a few weeks back I was surprised it made it up the steep hills in Redondo Beach.

"But your brother and sister aren't here yet. Don't you want to see them?" Now, my daddy knows they're notoriously late for family events if they show up at all.

"Tell them I said Merry Christmas and Happy New Year." I take my pile of food, kiss my stepmother good-bye, and head for the back door. I have to wait for my daddy to move the five cars blocking me in, but I'm ready to go, and he gets the message loud and clear.

"Okay, baby. I know you can't wait to show off your new ride," he says, taking a quick bite from his plate before passing it back to Faye to cover up until he gets back in. She's a good wife to put up with him and serve him like she does. Mama used to do that for Daddy, but he lost that privilege a long, long time ago. I'll have to tell Mama about my day when she gets in from volunteering at the shelter later, if she's not too tired. Otherwise I'll catch up with her at Netta's tomorrow. She has to drop off some hair products and I know she'll want to take a look at my hoopty when she does.

"Thanks again, Daddy, and Merry Christmas, everyone," I say to the whole lot of them without waiting for a reply. My dad's busy collecting keys to reorganize the cars. At least when my brother and sister arrive they'll have a good spot to park in.

Too bad I didn't bring my iPod to roll with. Maybe it's a good thing. I need to focus and get to know my car better. I also need to pay attention to the road and keep up with Rah, who arrives right on time.

"Hey, Mr. Jackson," Rah says from his open window. I can see Rahima in the backseat, knocked out. I guess she had a busy day at his grandparents' house. If I could go back to being two I'd do it in a heartbeat. She has no idea of the drama that swirls around her.

"Hey," my daddy says back to him. He's never liked Rah too much and the feeling between them is mutual. My daddy finally moves the last car out of my way. I wave to Rah and get in my car, fasten the seatbelt and say a quick prayer to Legba that I make it home safely. I start the engine, which takes a few seconds to turn over, and gently press the gas. The loud roar of the engine sounds like a fart and smells like one too.

"Are you sure this car is safe to drive?" I yell toward my daddy as he walks up the driveway, waiting for me to back out. He ignores my question and waves at me to get a move on. I know he wants to get back inside and rejoin the party and I just want to get a move on—period.

"I'll see you later, baby, and be safe," he says. I pull off and follow Rah. I can't wait to get to his crib and shake this day off in a real way.

By the time we arrive at my mom's house, my car's hotter than a chili pepper. I knew this car was a piece of shit and should've told my daddy so right then and there. He'll find some way to blame this on me and I'm not having it. I park the car in front of my mom's apartment building, where Rah's waiting patiently. If I'm lucky someone will jack this ride before sunrise. It's covered by my daddy's insurance until I get my own, so I'm not worried about the liability. I take my food out, slam the door, and hop in Rah's Acura, ready for a smooth ride.

"Hey, baby. How was your day?" Rah asks, pulling away from the curb and off toward his house. All the buildings on the block are lit up with pretty lights, and people are still outside hanging. This is how Christmas is supposed to be.

"It's better now," I say, turning around to greet his bundle of joy. "Hi, Rahima." I swear this little girl is the sweetest thing ever. "How was your holiday?"

"It was good, huh, little mama?" Rah answers for her. She smiles back at her daddy through the rearview mirror before initiating a game of hide-and-seek with me. "She's still hyped from all the sweets my grandparents gave her. We had a great time until my mom showed up." From the look on his face he doesn't want to go into too much detail. His mom's a trip and then some.

"No stripping on the holidays?"

"Nah, she's working later tonight, I'm sure. But she had to make an appearance with her new nigga and you know how that goes. So that's the car, huh," he says, eyeing my little bucket in his rearview. I'm sure he'll take a better look at it in the daylight, even if there's not much to see.

"Yup, that's it."

"Looks like it's overheating. You shouldn't drive it too far until I take a good look under the hood." How come Rah can look out for my well-being but my daddy can't?

"Well, I need to roll it to work tomorrow. You don't think it'll be okay to get to Compton and back?"

"I can't say. I just know what I smell, and it ain't good. I can take you to work if need be, Jayd. I'd rather that than you rolling around and get stuck somewhere. What was your dad thinking about, man? I wouldn't let Rahima ride around in that thing."

"Now you're just being cruel," I say, playfully pushing his shoulder. I know he's still irritated about Jeremy being over at Mama's yesterday, but that was Rah's bad, not mine.

"No, I'm just being truthful. But maybe your rich, white boyfriend will buy you something better." I knew that was coming. I turn away from Rahima and focus on Rah's chocolate skin. Maybe if he wasn't so fine I'd be able to leave him alone.

"Don't hate on Jeremy for being there when you couldn't be." I know he had to go get his daughter, but he had plans with me, and Sandy was just hating on his time. He needs to put her ass in check once and for all and we'd have a lot less drama between us.

"Is that how it's going to be, Jayd? Every time I can't make it somewhere you're going to call that punk to be your substitute?" Damn, I wish I'd driven my car, even if it is a death trap. It's better than being at his mercy for the rest of the evening.

"What the hell? I know you're not talking about someone looking for a replacement," I say, flicking the keychain picture of my crew at the Halloween Ball that hangs from my purse. I guess since Nellie isn't technically our homegirl anymore I should remove it, but I'm still hopeful she'll come around. There's no replacing a real friend. Now how can I make Rah understand that?

"Whatever, Jayd. You know that was wrong. Why can't you just admit it?" I look back at Rahima and ignore him for the time being. Part of me does feel bad, but I shouldn't. I just don't like seeing anyone I love hurt. But Rah brought this pain on himself. The rest of the short ride back to his house is quiet, except for Rahima's giggling and two-word sentences. Maybe we can play for the rest of the night while Rah sulks.

When we get in the house I immediately go into the studio and take Rahima with me while Rah goes to his room. Kamal stayed at their grandparents' house for the night so it's just the three of us chilling tonight.

"You hungry?" I ask her as I unwrap my food. Now I'm starving and ready to tear Faye's feast up. I take a forkful of macaroni and cheese and give it to Rahima. She smiles with delight and I know how she feels. I take the remote and turn on the flat-screen television.

"*Soul Food*'s on if you want to watch it," Rah says, entering the room a little more relaxed. I guess he didn't want to smoke around his daughter and for that I am glad. He also changed out of his jeans and dress shirt into some navy sweats and a black wife beater, ready to chill. I'm glad I'm already dressed comfortably.

"Yeah, that's one of my favorite movies." He looks at me cross, like he didn't know that already.

"Rah, you home?" his mother yells through the front door. What's she doing here? I know it's technically her house, but she's never home and it isn't good when she is.

"Yeah, we're back here," he says, taking a seat on the futon next to us.

"Oh, isn't this cozy," she says sarcastically. Rah's mother has never cared much for me and I can't stand her ass. She reminds me way too much of both Sandy and Trish. That's why I can't understand how Rah could pick those broads to deal with.

"Mom, what is it?"

"I need a sack. Kevin wants to smoke." What the hell? Please tell me his own mother isn't a client. That's just too trifling for me.

"Mom, not now. I'm busy."

"What, playing house? Jayd sweetie, don't get too comfortable. That baby ain't yours and neither is my son," she says with the venom of a rattlesnake on her tongue.

"Mom, not now." Rah's jaw tightens and so does his mother's. They look a lot alike in the face, but Rah has his father's large build.

"Come on, Rah. He's in the car waiting and we want to smoke before I go on stage. Hook me up." Rah reluctantly gets up and goes back to his room, leaving me alone with this broad. We stare at each other and keep our silence, or so I think.

"Rahima, you thirsty, mommy?" I say, picking her up and putting her in my lap to take a sip from the water bottle sitting on the table.

"Don't get too attached, Jayd. I'm warning you," she says, taking a sip out of the plastic cup in her hand. I can smell the hard liquor from here. "Consider it my gift to you." I look up at her and something tells me to listen to her warning, even if it is coming from a hateful place. Her voice gives me goose bumps. Rahima takes the water bottle from my hands and downs the drink. She then looks up at me and smiles big, ready for more food, and I'm happy to indulge the little princess.

"I'd think you'd be happy I'm nice to your granddaughter," I say, but I should know better than to give his mother any credit. She barely watches after her own children. She's probably never spent a day with her grandbaby. Mama would have a fit if she couldn't see me on a regular basis, and as she would put it, babies are a blessing not a burden.

"You can be nice to her all you want," Carla says, tugging at her too-tight and too-short mini skirt. Her halter top hardly covers her flat breasts but even I admit the rest of her body is fierce. I guess working at a strip club all week keeps her in shape. "Just remember what I said."

"Why do you care?" I don't mean to be rude but she's never had too much to say to me before now. I continue to focus on Rahima, who's now rubbing her tired eyes and chewing simultaneously. She'll be knocked out soon with a full tummy. What a life this little girl has.

"I don't, not really. But you know Sandy's just teasing my son with that little girl. I know the game, sweetie. And if you think you, Rah, and that baby are going to be one big happy family you're more delusional than I thought you were." Carla takes another sip from her cup and looks over her shoulder. What's taking Rah so long? He knows this woman works my nerves.

"Who said anything like that?" Rahima takes the plastic fork from me and starts feeding herself as well as she can with her tiny hands. I guess I'm not moving fast enough for her. "She's a sweet little girl and I happen to like kids."

"Tell me you don't have dreams about that little baby being

yours." After a moment of silence, I look up at Carla, who hasn't stopped staring at me for a moment. I guess she's waiting for an answer and I'm not in the mood for her at all.

"For your information, I'm still a virgin, so it's not even possible for me and Rah to have a baby." Maybe that'll shut her up.

"You think you're slick, trying to be all sweet and shit. Bitches always win, honey. Always." So much for wishful thinking. I now see she'll never shut up about this.

"I'm not trying to be or do anything but feed the baby so she can get a good night's sleep. Isn't this actually more your job than mine?"

"Yeah, so you should ask yourself why you're volunteering to do it when I'm not." She got me there. Even my mom warned me about getting too close to Rahima. "Would you be here if that little baby wasn't?" That sounded too familiar, but not from my own memories. I'll have to remember to ask Mama about that one tomorrow when I see her at Netta's shop.

"Here. Bye," Rah says, throwing the small plastic bag at his now happy mother, and not a moment too soon. She can really work a nerve.

"Bye," she says, and walks out as quickly as she walked in and I'm glad she's finally gone. At least now we can relax and enjoy the movie before falling asleep, because she just drained us all. But I am happy to be here. And whether or not Rahima's the bigger reason is of no consequence to me. I like her and her daddy and I don't see anything wrong with that. This is the most joy I've felt all day and I wouldn't trade it for anything in the world.

~ 5 ~
Sweet Tooth

"Who got they own flow/
Who ain't looking for/
Who sugar no more."

—CHRISSETTE MICHELE

*"*I *love you, Jayd. Why can't you see that?" Jeremy asks, holding on to me as I stand suspended in midair. I should be falling into the abyss below, but I'm not. Instead, I'm secure in Jeremy's hands yet I still have the impulse to run.*

"Jeremy, I can't stay. You're in danger." Before I can finish my thought, Rah appears out of nowhere wearing the same suit my great-grandfather wore in my daydream with Mama. What the hell?

"Back up, fool. Jayd's my girl," Rah says, snatching my free hand and pulling me toward him. I feel like I'm in a tug of war. "We belong together. Tell this punk to step off, Jayd, before someone gets hurt." Jeremy, unmoved by Rah's threats, holds my other hand tighter and pulls me hard in his direction.

"You're hurting me," I say to both of them. "For real, let me go." Neither of them honors my request and I stay in the middle, being pulled back and forth between the two of them. My arms feel like they're going to snap out of their sockets. I can hear a baby crying in the background, momentarily distracting me from my uncomfortable situation.

It sounds like Rahima. I turn around looking for her, but I can't see where the sound is coming from.

"Jayd, hold on to the rope," my mom says, appearing in my dream. "Whatever you do, don't let go. You are all you can depend on to stay up." Just then, both boys let me go and I begin to fall.

"Jayd, hold on," my mom shouts, but I can't see a thing. I'm falling and gaining speed the farther I drop. I don't see a rope anywhere, but I'm not scared. On the way down I notice I have Rahima wrapped on my back like our ancestors carried their babies. I look back at her and she's now sound asleep. She trusts me to keep her safe and that's exactly what I intend to do.

"Give me my baby," Sandy shouts from the bottom of the pit. Finally the rope appears above my head but now I'm falling so fast that I can't catch it. Sandy's at the bottom with a huge catcher's mitt on her right hand and she's socking it like a professional baseball player.

"I got this one," Sandy says. I look around the bottom of the pit and see it's in the shape of a diamond, like a baseball field. What kind of game is this, where I'm the ball? I see Laura, Misty, Nellie, and Tania in the outfield, also with mitts on, but it's Sandy who's going to get me caught up. I can't stop myself from falling right into her arms.

"No!" I yell. I reach harder for the rope and barely touch it with the tip of my fingers. With Rahima on my back I have to work hard to do something that normally would have been easy.

"If you let Rahima go you'll get farther and then you can go back for her, Jayd." My mom's right but I can't let her go. I struggle to reach for the rope but it's no use. I'm now falling through clouds and soon I'll be within Sandy's reach.

"Jayd," Rah calls out to me from the top of the abyss. I

can see now that he's the one who threw me the rope. Jeremy
looks over Rah's shoulder but they're both completely help-
less. I look back at Rahima, who's now wide awake and
looking down at her mother. She starts to cry and I try to
comfort her by patting her back, but it's no use. We look at
each other and realize there's nothing I can do to save her.

Before I land in Sandy's hands, she steps aside and lets
me crash. The moment my stomach hits the ground the
change in my pockets falls out and the other girls swoop in
to scoop it up. I'm paralyzed from the waist down, but luck-
ily Rahima's fine. Sandy smiles as she steps over me, staring
down at my crippled body. She snatches Rahima from my
back and disappears.

"Jayd, I trusted you," Rah yells down at me. As I glance
up I can see the disappointment written all over Rah's face
and even worse, Jeremy has the same look.

"Stuntin' is a habit, put it in da air." David Banner's ring-
tone wakes me up from my nightmarish dream just in time. I
never want to think about losing Rahima again. I pick up the
phone and flip it open without looking at the Caller ID.

"Hello."

"Good morning, Jayd. How was your Christmas?" What
time is it? If Jeremy's calling me I know it must be late. I look
around Rah's den and notice that he and Rahima are
nowhere to be found. I hope her daddy's got her because to
let my dream tell it, I certainly don't.

"It was cool," I say, groggily coming to consciousness. I'm
not sure what time it is but it feels late to me. I want to get at
least five hours of work in at the shop today, so I'd better get
a move on. "I got a car," I say, unenthusiastically revealing the
most important gift of all, or so I think. Just then I notice a
small, wrapped box on the coffee table with the words
"Happy Kwanza" written across the thin paper. I sit up and

reach for the gift like I reached for the rope in my dream. Sometimes I wish I could forget my dreams once I wake up, but no chance of that happening anytime soon: one of the many blessings of being born with a caul over my face.

"A car? Well I guess you did have a merry Christmas after all." Jeremy's first car was a classic Mustang that's been in his family for generations and his next one is likely to be a brand new BMW. I would be excited too if that were the case, but not for me.

"Not really, but like I said, it was cool. What's up with you?" I stand up and stretch my right arm above my head, ready to get on with this day. There's money to be made and I'm letting it slip from my hands the longer I sit and chill.

"Well, my parents are going skiing for a couple of days and I just wanted to know if you wanted to come over tonight for pizza and a movie. Nothing fancy, and I'll be good, I promise."

"Promises, promises," I say. I hear the front door open and know it's time to go. Rah will know instantly by my body language that it's Jeremy on the phone and I'm not in the mood to argue, especially not with an unclaimed gift on the table.

"Is that an affirmative answer, Miss Jackson?" Jeremy asks, making me smile early in my day. And after my disturbing dream I need some comic relief.

"Sure, why not," I say, kicking the fleece socks off my feet and under my bag on the floor. It should be a good money-making day with all of the sisters needing repair to their holiday hairdos. Between now and the six days until New Year's I should make some pretty decent cash. That's all the motivation I need to get up and out.

"Well, don't sound so enthusiastic about it," he says, a bit insulted by my response.

"I'm sorry, I didn't mean it like that. I had a long day and my car is busted and I just got it. So, I'll still need a ride tonight."

"Not a problem, Lady J. I'm always happy to be your escort." Jeremy's so sweet, sometimes I feel bad for not wanting to be his girlfriend again. Rah walks into the studio with Rahima in one arm and her sippy cup in his free hand. He looks at me and I know I have to go. I don't want to start our morning off on the wrong foot.

"I'll hit you later," I say, rushing off the phone.

"Alright. Don't work too hard," Jeremy says before hanging up. Damn, that was close.

"Good morning," Rah says, kissing me on the cheek. I open my arms to take Rahima, who'd rather walk around this morning from the way she just jumped out of her daddy's arms and hit the ground running.

"Oh, so it's like that," I say to her. She smiles big and runs up to me, hugging me tightly before running off in the other direction toward her toy blocks across the room. Rah looks at his daughter and smiles.

"You see that? She's already got skills. Wait until I get her out on the court. She's going to ball all over those fools," he says, balling up a piece of paper and tossing it up in the air like a basketball for Rahima to catch the rebound, which she does.

"Wow, I see skills are hereditary." As if I don't know about inheriting gifts. We look at each other and smile at Rahima's excitement from catching the paper ball. I wish everything in life were so easy. I'm still disturbed from the dream I just awoke from but I'm not ready to talk about it yet, especially not with Rah.

"Did you see your Kwanza gift?" Rah passes me the small box I noticed a few minutes ago.

"I didn't know it was for me." I take the box from him and open it to find a brand new cell phone inside. "How did you know I needed this?"

"I didn't really. I just figured it's time for you to get an up-grade." This is why Rah's my boy for life. He can always anticipate what I need right when I need it.

"Oh Rah, I love it. Thank you," I say, hugging him tightly before taking my gift out of the box. This is better than my car.

"You're welcome," he says, picking up Rahima and walking back into the kitchen. It's a pink Razor, just what I wanted. I follow them out of the studio and take a picture of them both to save on my phone. Rah walks over, looks at the photo and smiles.

"Nice picture, huh?" Before answering, he passes the baby to me and takes my phone, repeating my action.

"Now that's a nice picture to me." Before we can relish in the sweetness of the moment any longer the doorbell rings and someone starts knocking loudly. It must be Sandy, here to pick up their daughter. No one else would be that rude this early in the day.

"Damn, she's early," Rah says, reluctantly leaving the kitchen to answer the door.

"What the hell took you so long to answer? My nigga's in the car waiting for us. We're on our way back to Pomona," she says without so much as a hello. "And what is that bitch doing holding my baby?" Why is she calling me by her nickname, especially in front of her daughter? "Here baby, look what mommy brought you," she says, snatching an upset Rahima from my arms and giving her a lollipop for breakfast.

"Why do you have to be so rude, Sandy? We were just about to feed her a real breakfast instead of that crap you're always giving her," Rah says, standing next to me.

"Whatever. Where's her bag and car seat? We have to go,"

she says, unwrapping the candy and stuffing it in her daughter's mouth. Her daughter reluctantly takes it but she looks like she still wants to cry. Sandy's a poster model for unfit parenting if there ever was one.

"You're an hour early. I'm not rushing," Rah says, taking Rahima away from her mother before heading to the back to get her stuff and leaving me and his prodigal baby-mama alone. What the hell? He should know better than that. Sandy props herself against the kitchen counter, crossing one high heel over the other.

"So, are you two having fun playing house with my baby?" Sandy looks like a hooker on a good day and a slut on a bad one. What did Rah ever see in her? What did I ever see in her? After all, she was my friend first.

"Rahima's his daughter too, or did you forget that magical night under the bleachers three years ago when he was my man?"

"Shut the hell up, Jayd. That's always been your problem: too much talking and not enough doing. Men like action, or haven't you noticed?" she says, shifting her weight from one stiletto to the other while crossing her arms over her large breasts. At least she's got some meat on her bones, unlike Trish.

"Apparently not, because I'm still here and you're not."

"I'll always be here. Remember, I have his baby, Jayd. You couldn't get rid of me if you wanted to, and I know you're not giving him any because that's what Trish is for, or have you conveniently forgotten about her?" If this trick keeps talking to me out the side of her face I'm going to have to slap it back in place.

"I'm not worried about either one of y'all. And unlike the two of you, I have better things to do with my time than run after a dude with my legs wide open." Sandy shoots me an evil look but she can't say shit. She's knows I'm right. I walk past her and into the kitchen to start breakfast. From the looks of his groceries Rah's making grits, eggs, toast, and turkey bacon. I'll get started on the grits now because I know he's real particular about how he likes his eggs scrambled.

"This little sweet act you've got going on will only get you so far, Jayd," Sandy says, following me around the kitchen. "To keep a man you'll eventually have to take off that chastity belt you're wearing and let a nigga in." She sounds just like Rah's mom. No wonder he's oddly attracted to her.

"Sandy, if I want your advice I'll ask for it." I'm trying to keep a cool head but this trick is making it very hard. Rah left me alone last night with his mom and now this morning with Sandy. Does he want me to slap one of these broads or what?

"No you won't, but you should take it. Trust, Jayd. The way to get to Rah can't be found on that stove."

"Little do you know," I say, thinking of all the times Rah and I have been in the kitchen together. "Like I said before, I'm still here and you're not, no matter how loud you get about it. Now if you'll excuse me, I have breakfast to cook before I go to work. You know that place you go to make money for yourself instead of always having your hand out begging? You should try it out someday."

"Oh I works for mine, sweetie. You best believe it," she says, looking out of the window and toward the green Ford Explorer parked in the driveway. It looks like it was in an accident recently. I hope they buckle in Rahima correctly.

"Jayd, I told you not to worry about that baby. Her mama's standing right there. Let her worry about that."

"Did you hear the crap this girl is talking about? She's not concerned about her daughter's well-being, and since I'm here I can't help but be worried."

"Jayd, I'm telling you, as sweet as that little girl is, she can bring you an equal amount of pain, just like having a sweet tooth. It seems like a good idea at first to eat the en-

*tire value pack of Now and Laters until you get a toothache,
which leads to a root canal or maybe even the loss of a
tooth. Take it from me, Jayd, and heed my warning. Let the
parents parent. You be a friend and nothing more. You have
enough responsibility as it is."*

"Where's Karl? Shouldn't y'all be enjoying breakfast in
bed or something?"

"*Who says we're not?*" And with that last visual my mom's
out and I'm back to reality.

"Jayd, what the hell is wrong with you? You still act strange,
you know that?"

"Sandy, can't you wait outside? I'm sure your man is
lonely." Speaking of the devil, he blows his horn impatiently
and I know Rah won't like that at all.

"I know that nigga didn't just honk at me," Rah says, walking in from the back of the house and back into the foyer,
with Rahima right next to him. He rarely lets her feet touch
the ground, but sometimes she insists and I don't blame her.
It's nice to be able to stand on your own two feet sometimes.

"Well maybe if you hurried your ass up some then he
wouldn't have to honk. I told you we're in a rush."

"This is my daughter, not his. You better tell that fool
something," Rah says, looking out of the window at the
dude. Now that I have a car I'm still stuck in situations I don't
want to be in. What's wrong with this picture?

"*And I told you your daddy wouldn't come through,
right? So don't beat yourself up for too long about trusting
him. You should be able to depend on him but sometimes
life ain't fair, as I'm sure you know. Just stay on your grind,
Jayd, and all will be fine. Focus on you, baby.*"

"I thought you were gone," I say, but I'm glad she's in my
head. I need her to keep me from blowing up. This holiday
has sucked entirely, and I can't believe I'm saying this, but
I'm ready to go back to school.

"Soon enough, Jayd. I'll be out of your head when you get the message. You can only control your own actions, and right now all of your movements need to be focused on getting you to where you want to be." In and out of my dream, my mom's right. I need to keep it moving and get up out of here as soon as I can. This drama is giving me a headache and ultimately it has nothing to do with me.

"There she goes again," Sandy says, rolling her eyes at me. "Rah, I don't want Jayd and her strangeness affecting my daughter."

"She's our daughter and you're the strangest one of all," he says. I appreciate him defending me, but he shouldn't talk down about Sandy in front of their daughter. That's not good at all. Maybe if I remove myself from the situation it'll be better for everyone and I can start right now. He was cooking breakfast initially and he can finish it. I've got to get ready for work. We can still make it by eleven, and that'll give me a good six hours to make some serious cash.

"I'm going to take a shower and get ready for work. Can you still drop me off?"

"Yeah, and I'll take a look at your car when I get back. Just leave the keys with me."

"Car? If you got a car why do you need dropping off?" Why is Sandy all up in my business this morning? We haven't had this much communication in years and she's wearing me out. She's definitely from the same tribe of ashe stealers as my daddy's folks, I swear.

"Sandy, mind your business. Jayd, I'm going to walk Rahima out," he says, making it clear to me and Sandy that she's not a part of his equation, and I know that's not going to settle well in Sandy's mind. No matter how many dudes she may roll with, I know in the end she only wants Rah.

I decide to take my time in the shower this morning to make sure the coast is clear of Sandy and her madness. By the time I finish getting ready, Sandy and Rahima are gone and Rah's on the phone in deep conversation with someone.

"Alright, ma'am. I'll be sure to get you all of the info on Monday morning. Thanks again," he says, hanging up.

"Hey, is this for me?" I uncover the warm plate to find a breakfast fit for a queen, complete with orange slices. I love it when he cooks.

"But of course. You need a healthy meal to start your day off right." Rah steps behind me at the counter and reaches onto the plate, picking up an orange slice and putting it up to my lips for me to take a bite.

"Thank you," I say, nervously. Whenever he gets too close my body heat rises and this is not the time for it.

"What time you getting off?" Damn, I know he's going to want to kick it with me tonight if he picks me up from Netta's, and he'll be hella suspicious if I say I don't need a ride.

"I'm not sure yet but I'll call you when I find out."

"Yeah, and we have to get your phone switched over so maybe we can do that later, too." Why is he all of a sudden making definite plans with me for the whole day? What's really going on?

"Sounds good," I say, walking back toward the bathroom to make sure I didn't forget anything. I'm so used to carrying around all of my stuff that it's second nature to me by now to always do a once-over before leaving wherever I happen to be.

"The attorney said I have a good chance at winning custody, especially with Sandy's history." I hope Rah's right, for everyone's sake. If my dream is any indication of his reaction to losing Rahima again, I don't want to be anywhere around if it happens.

"I hope he's right," I say.

"But a little backup wouldn't hurt."

"Oh no, Rah. I'm not getting involved with this one," I say. "The last potion I made for you didn't take, and I'm not trying anything else, especially not for something this serious."

"Who says it didn't take? Trish ain't feeling me like she was, no matter what she says and, well, Sandy's just crazy so you can't count her. You have to be patient, baby. Haven't you learned that by now?"

"No, I guess I haven't. Well, there is a chocolate brownie recipe that's supposed to help sway the law in your favor." I remember seeing it in the spirit book when I was looking for something else. "I just remember it having a lot of brown sugar in it and I know how you hate sweets."

"If you make it I'll love it. And you know brown sugar's my favorite," he says, turning me around and pulling me in close to him, kissing my lips like only he can.

"I'll see what I can do," I say, giving in to his request. Maybe Mama would be willing to help me with this one.

By the time we get to Netta's Never Nappy Beauty Shop, her usual Saturday clients are already in the washbowl having their heads washed. Mama's also in the back working on their hair products. When she has a lot to do for the shop, she'd rather make it all here than have to lug the products from our house. She'll be in and out without Netta's other clients seeing her, and that's just how Mama likes it. Christmas and Kwanza wipe our supply of products out every year, and Mama and Netta make a killing on their gift baskets, but I never know exactly how much Mama makes. She keeps her money to herself and I don't blame her.

"Jayd, the sweetest thing in the world is a baby," Mama says while I mix together my concoction. I need a new braid spray and this should do the trick. I'm working on the rest of my hair products too, paying special attention to the needs of clients with cornrows. "Especially if you don't have to deliver it."

"Now ain't that the truth," Netta says, walking in on our conversation. All of her clients are now under the blow-dryers for the next fifteen minutes or so, depending on their style, leaving her free to chat with us. "I loved each of your Mama's babies when they were babies. That's when they can do no wrong. But they do grow up, Jayd. And until then, they come with grown-ups of their own when they're as little this little bottle of sunshine," Netta says, passing my new phone to Mama and displaying the picture of Rahima and me.

"Netta, what are you doing going through my stuff?" I reach for the phone but when Mama looks at me like I've lost my mind, I step back and let them eye my present from Rah.

"Well isn't this nice," Mama says, inspecting my new cell like a DEA agent. "And the picture is so sweet."

"Isn't it?" Netta takes control of stirring our new hair concoction for the time being. "They make a nice little family, don't they? Too bad you and Rah are too young to get married." Not in some states, but I'm not stupid enough to say it out loud and I pray my mother's not listening.

"This baby is surrounded by a bunch of teenage fools—no offense," Mama says, looking into my eyes. "Jayd, what did you dream about last night?" Damn, now she can read me when I have dreams too? I think her lock on me has gotten stronger since our shared vision on Christmas Eve. I guess there's no sense in lying to her.

"I dreamt I lost Rahima to Sandy, and Rah hated me. But I think it was because of something his mom said to me last night."

"What did she say?" Mama asks.

"She said that sweet girls never win."

"Oh, that's not true. It may seem like that initially but truth be told, it's the sweet girls that win in the end. Bitches wear their asses and everyone else's out eventually." Netta's a trip. She walks to the door and peeks out her head to check on her clients, who are deeply engrossed in their gossip columns and tightly tucked under their dryers.

"Did you say you lost the baby?" Mama's so observant I think that she's missed her calling as a CSI agent. With their skills combined, Mama and Netta make a formidable team.

"Yeah. I was falling and Rahima was on my back and Sandy snatched her from me once I hit the ground. I also lost some change, which was weird. I've never dreamt about money before."

"Then that should be your first priority, right, Lynn Mae?" Netta stops stirring the sweet-scented liquid and stares at my grandmother, who's deep in thought.

"Yes, it should. Anything that stands out as new in your dreams should be paid the most attention to. Have you been saving your money?"

"Aside from the fifteen dollars I have in my purse now, I have a little stashed away for my car."

"What about in the bank?" I look at Mama and smile.

"Why would I have a bank account?" The only teenagers I know with bank accounts are the rich ones at school, Jeremy of course included. Everyone else uses a sock drawer or piggy bank, like me.

"Girl, what is your mother thinking?" I guess this was a topic of conversation between the two of them some time ago.

"Mmhmm," Netta says, wiping her hands dry and looking at the clock. It's time for us to get back to our clients and I'm anxious to make some tips.

"Jayd, your mother was supposed to teach you how to manage your money properly and open you an account by the time you were fifteen. It's taboo for a child of Oshune to be frivolous with her money. And now that you have money coming in you have no time to waste." Mama hands me my phone and takes over mixing the hair spray I thought up. "We'll talk about Rah later. Right now we have to finish our work and then you and I are going straight to the bank. Lucky for you they don't close until five and the bank manager's a client of mine. You're opening an account today before the sun sets."

"Mama, can we do this tomorrow? I have plans tonight." Which reminds me, I need to send Rah a text saying I won't be able to hang out tonight. I take my old cell out of my pocket and quickly send Rah the message.

"Jayd, you'll go around taking care of other people's needs before protecting your own interests. And as sweet as that sounds in theory, it's not a very smart move in reality." Well, I guess I'm going to the bank with Mama. Now I really don't know how I'm getting back to Inglewood tonight. Maybe Jeremy will be up for coming to get me from Mama's now that he's been all the way to my house, although I don't want to make a habit of intertwining my neighborhood business and school business.

After the last client leaves seven hours later, we clean up and get ready to roll to the bank. Too bad my car's not here. I would've driven Mama and me up the road, but she probably wouldn't have gotten in the car with me anyway.

"You two better go on and get. You've only got ten minutes before the bank closes and it'll take you at least that long to get there on foot," Netta says.

"I'm just glad they opened that new branch off of Long Beach Boulevard. Before that I had to go all the way to South Bay to go to the bank," Mama says.

"Well, you know how they are about our money. They want it but will be damned if they make it convenient for us to give it to them." Netta and Mama have been complaining about that fact of black life for a long time. In Redondo Beach, there's a bank or teller machine on damn-near every corner. In Compton and Inglewood there's a check-cashing place on every corner. But some banks are getting better about having multiple branches in our hoods.

"Alright, Netta. Jayd will make it up to you tomorrow, won't you, baby?" Mama winks at me and walks toward the front door, purse and coat in hand. I guess I'm moving too slow for her. I see she's serious about me getting my money in the bank. I've got to read about this taboo in my lessons. There are so many stories about Oshune's various taboos that I can barely keep up with them, just like the rules of being a priestess. They have no real order; just the one Mama gives them. And I never remember what that is.

As we walk up Alondra toward Long Beach Boulevard, I can barely keep up with Mama. She called before we left to make sure they keep the doors open till closing time, but the banks are always busy during the holidays anyway and I'm willing to bet there are still people in line. When we hit the front door, I can see I should've bet twenty dollars. There are five people in front of us and the security guard locks the doors behind us, making it clear we're the last customers. Since it looks like we're going to be in line for a while, this is a good time to ask for her advice about dealing with Rah's drama.

"So, I think I'm supposed to help Rah keep Rahima, but I'm not sure if I can," I say to Mama as we wait for the next teller.

"Did Rah ask you for your help?"

"Yes, he did."

"Then you have a choice to make. Helping him isn't an obligation and you should be very careful not to get hurt in the crossfire that will most definitely come." We look at the Christmas lights shining bright in the early evening hour. Maybe it can be my gift to him and bring us all closer together. That would be the sweetest thing ever. "And remember, this isn't about you, Rah, or Sandy. It's about the baby, and that's where your good ashe needs to be focused, little one."

"Well, I saw a brownie recipe in the spirit book, for gaining good luck with the law. You think that'll work?"

"Yes, and you should also put a little sweet water in for the good luck of the baby. That'll be a sure winner," Mama says, her green eyes glistening as she winks at me. Netta did Mama's hair last week, per her usual Tuesday appointment, and it still looks immaculate.

"That's in the spirit book?"

"Yes, right in the middle of the Potions and Tinctures section. But I'll have to help you make it. You need all the positive ashe you can get to make it work right, especially under these circumstances."

"Good evening, Mrs. James. How's your holiday season going?" one of the tellers behind the counter asks Mama.

"Everything's just fine, Mary. How's your family doing? And I see you've been using the hair cream I made for you." Mama takes out her bankcard and swipes it in the machine.

"They're all fine and yes, I'm loving it," she says, instinctively touching her shoulder-length curls. Anyone with eyes can tell she's feeling good about her hair from the way she's throwing it over her shoulders and smiling bright. Mama's touch can do that to anyone. "I can't thank you enough."

"Anytime, Mary. And this is my oldest granddaughter, Jayd." I wave at the lady and she looks at me and smiles big, but her eyes tell me she's also wondering if I have the same touch Mama does. "We're here to open her a checking account, and I also want to check my balance while I'm here." Without hesitation, Mary prints out Mama a receipt and turns her attention toward me.

"Well, young lady, there's no charge to open up a checking account and you'll also have a savings account attached to it. Here's your balance, Mrs. James." She hands the paper to Mama, who reads it quickly. She then reaches down to put the paper into her bag but it falls to the floor instead.

"I got it," I say, bending down to retrieve the small square. I glance at the total and almost choke on my own spit. Mama's been holding out on a sistah, for real.

"Thank you," she says, taking the paper from my hand, my mouth wide open. "Okay, Mary, can we withdraw one hundred from my checking account to open up Jayd's account, and then deposit whatever she has on her? Merry Christmas, Jayd."

"Thank you," I say, still shocked at the amount of dough Mama's sitting on. She's not a millionaire, but in our hood they'd still think she was the shit.

"Of course, Mrs. James. It won't take long. Let me go get the paperwork and meet you both at one of the tables." She points to a seating area behind us and we walk over to a desk with three chairs around it to wait for Mary.

"Jayd, my money is my business, you hear?" Mama whispers, taking one of the two seats next to each other.

"Of course. But Mama, you could have your own house." I sit next to her, ready to grill her.

"I do, and I'm not leaving it because of your grandfather, your uncles, or anyone else. If you take care of your money Oshune will always bless you with more. That's why she likes sweetness, Jayd. During the hard times remember what's sweetest about life and you'll never be broke, no matter how it may look on the outside."

"Okay, well how about hooking me up with some new gear?" I tease, but Mama doesn't find me amusing.

"It's not an asset if you can wear it on your ass. Remember that." She's right. It doesn't matter what it may look like to anyone else, what we have is more valuable than any outfit I can buy, although I wouldn't mind having a new wardrobe. But that'll have to wait until my ride is solid. Living like the rich kids I go to school with must be a different experience altogether, and not all good.

By the time Mama and I finish hooking up my new account and walk home, it's almost six and Jeremy should be pulling up anytime. I step outside of the spirit room, where Mama and I ended up looking through the spirit book, and walk to the front yard right in time for Jeremy.

"Hey, Jayd. You look tired," Jeremy says, unlocking the doors so I can join him.

"I am. I've been working all day and then I had to go to the bank with my grandmother. I don't think I'll be able to stay awake through a movie."

"Well, I'll just settle for taking you home tonight. But you owe me," he says, reaching over my head and into the backseat to reveal a large shopping bag.

"Jeremy, I thought we were over the gift-buying part of our friendship," I say as he puts the big bag on my lap and smiles proudly. He just can't help himself, I guess.

"It's a necessity, not a luxury. And besides, it's still Christmas. Open it."

"Since when do you celebrate religious holidays?" I ask as I play with the tissue paper inside of the bag. It looks expensive, whatever it is, which makes me even more curious.

"Hey, I'm no Scrooge. I love Christmas." I look down at the bag, unsure if I want to open it or just put it back in the backseat. Noticing my apprehension, Jeremy takes my left hand and places it inside the bag. "Now come on, what kind of friend would you be if you denied me the gift of giving? Isn't that what this holiday's all about?" I look into Jeremy's blue eyes and give in. He can be very persuasive when he wants to be.

"I love it," I say, taking the soft, pink North Face jacket out of the bag and holding it up against my chest. I know this jacket must've cost at least two hundred, easily. He's gone way over the limit with this one. But I still like the way the fleece feels up against my skin.

"And I love that you love it." He smiles at my astonishment and kisses me on the nose before continuing toward my mother's house.

"Jeremy, I can't accept this. I've already told you not to buy me any more gifts, especially not gifts that are so expensive." As if controlled by some other force, I slip the jacket on, one arm at a time, and wrap myself up in its warmth. Damn, this feels too good.

"And I've told you that friends get gifts too, especially on the holidays." He looks at me and laughs at my indecisiveness. He knows I'm not parting ways with this jacket.

"As you shouldn't, girl," my mom intrudes. *"You better keep that jacket and make it last a long, long time. And don't even think about feeling bad. He's a good friend, Jayd, who wants nothing but friendship in return."*

"Thanks for the advice, mom," I think back. She always has a way of adding her two cents at just the right time.

"Well, I don't know what to say, Jeremy. This is really a nice gift."

"A simple thank you will suffice," he says, merging onto the highway with the rest of the evening traffic.

"Thank you."

"You're welcome." Jeremy looks down at his buzzing cell, chooses to ignore it, and then focuses back on the road. I still haven't taken my eyes off of my gift.

"I didn't get you anything." I put the jean jacket I've been sporting all day across my lap. It's okay to wear during the day, and as long as I'm layered up at night and not at the beach, I don't freeze completely. But this pink cutie will work no matter where I am or what I have on underneath.

"And I don't want you to. I saw it and thought it would look good on you and it does," he says, eyeing me as I stare at my reflection in the sun visor's mirror. He's right: this jacket suits me perfectly. Who am I to say I'm not worth it?

"How much did this set you back?" I know it's rude to ask, but I have to know. I didn't ask Rah how much the cell cost because he's always spent money on me, but with a one-hundred-dollar limit because we live on budgets. But Jeremy's spending has no cap and I want to know if this was on sale or what.

"I'm going to pretend like I didn't just hear that," Jeremy says, exiting the freeway. "Maybe we can do movie night at your mom's if she doesn't mind. I won't keep you up too late. I know you've got to work in the morning." He's right about that. I'm going to hustle hard this next week and stack up my chips. My car needs major work and if I'm going to keep it I have to be prepared for the cost. I also want to have money in the bank like Mama does. She has enough to roll out whenever it gets to be too much for her, but I know she's not rolling anytime soon. Just the fact that she can makes her that much more powerful, in my eyes, and I want that kind of freedom in my hands too.

~ 6 ~
Get Money

"Why white folks focus on dogs and yoga/
While people on the low end trying to ball and get over."

—COMMON

Ican't believe my vacation from school is coming to an end.
It's gone by so quickly, but I've learned more in these two
weeks with Netta and Mama than I have being in school for
the past four months. When we get back next week it'll be
the end of the semester and that means finals and term papers. I was going to work on my Califia paper for government class a little more this week, but between the shop and
my own clients I haven't had a moment to myself. It's already
Wednesday and I have enough work lined up to last the rest
of the week.

Mama and Netta have kept me busy both in the shop and
in the spirit room. Mama and I have come up with a potion
to help Rah, sweet water and all. I baked it into fudge brownies and he ate the entire batch in one sitting, which he would
normally never do. Him having the munchies helped out,
too. I just hope it's enough to make the law be sweet to him
and give him custody of his daughter, or at least shared custody. Mama said we can't ask for things out of selfishness because ultimately what's in the best interest of the client is all
that matters. And as far as Mama's concerned, Rahima's the
client and Rah and I are just acting on his daughter's behalf.

I've been driving my hoopty back and forth to work, and

with Rah's help it's been staying pretty cool, but is still not completely fixed. It's going to take more money to make it run smooth. I still need a few items for school, and even with my car expenses, I should be able to spend some of my hard-earned money on keeping my gear tight. Mickey and I decided to hit up Lakewood Mall because it's closer to Compton than the one in the South Bay and it's a good place for us to meet after work. Rah and Nigel are also meeting us a little later when they get finished balling at the local park.

"Jayd, what do you think of this dress?" Mickey holds up the baby outfit and I have to say, it is cute.

"I think it's adorable and expensive," I say, also eyeing the price tag. "Is she getting a job straight out of the womb or what?"

"Nickey Shantae will never have to want for anything and deserves to rock it like mommy and daddy do," she says, putting the pricey ensemble across her arm and waddling on down the aisle. Mickey is too much sometimes.

"Mickey, you don't even know if it's a girl yet."

"Yes, I do. Mothers just know, Jayd, even if it would make Nigel happy to have a boy. But he'll have to wait until next time."

"No comment," I say, not wanting to ruin our shopping day. I'll let her live in her knocked-up version of a fairy tale a little longer. But eventually my girl's going to have to wake up. If Nellie were here she'd be on reality alert. But it's just me, and I don't want to be the one to throw salt in her game. It's been a long workday and the rest of the week promises to only get longer with New Year's being Friday.

"So what are y'all doing for New Year's?"

"I'm going to be at home. It's a tradition for me and Mama to spend it together." Especially now. Mama had a dream about violence again and insists we bring in the New Year at the family shrine. And after my dream about falling to the ground with Rahima on my back, I'm with Mama completely on this one. "How about you? Are you and Nigel hanging out?"

"No. His family wants him to ring in the New Year at church. I want to go but I don't think they'll be too happy to see me there."

"What about your man? Don't y'all usually have a cookout at your house?"

"Yeah, but I'm not feeling that this year. I want to hang with my boo." Mickey looks down at her growing belly and I think I actually see tears in her eyes. I feel for my girl and her baby. She's managed to get herself into quite a tense situation, with no end in sight.

"Mickey, then go. Maybe if you show up they'll be alright with it. You never know until you try." A cute, yellow overall set catches my eye. That'll look so cute on Rahima.

"Yeah, maybe. But I don't want to get into it with his parents anymore. I want to win them over and I don't think I can do it in the two days we have left until New Year's."

"Mickey, this is a new side of you. You usually could give a damn about what people think of you, and that's an understatement."

"I know. It's pathetic, right?"

"No, not really. If you're really digging him, of course you want to be in with the family, depending on the family." In my case, I wish both Rah and Jeremy's folks didn't know me sometimes.

"And you know I'm really digging Nigel if I care about what his parents think of me. I can't help smiling when I think about him." And I know how sprung she feels. Every time I'm around Rah I cheese bigger than all outside, so I really can't say shit when it comes to her being in love with Nigel.

"Yeah, I know how you feel." Rah gets to me like no other

dude ever has, not even Jeremy. But Jeremy does come close. I think if Rah asked me to be his one and only girl I would sacrifice Jeremy to do so, but we'd always be friends. Lucky for me and Jeremy Rah's nowhere near ready for that kind of commitment. He is acting a little more clingy lately, but I think it's just because of the baby. Out of nowhere, Mickey starts bawling and making that ugly crying face I can't stand.

"Why do I feel so bad every time I'm not with Nigel? This can't be love if it hurts like this," Mickey whines as she continues shopping through her tears. For her and Nigel's wallet's sake, I hope it's a girl. Between this shopping spree and the one she went on last week, if it's not a girl they'll have some serious exchanging to do. And most of the stuff she's buying is on sale, so I'm not sure if they'll be able to get their money back. "I never felt this way with my man and we've been together since junior high. He was my first and everything, but he can't touch Nigel right now."

"Love always hurts," I say, remembering Maman getting beat down by her husband in front of her daughter and lover. Talk about pain. "If it doesn't hurt at some point it ain't the real thing."

"Damn, Jayd. When did you become so bitter? I thought you were the hopeless romantic of our crew."

"If you haven't noticed, our crew is down to two, and neither one of us is in the best position to be all romantic about life, now are we?" Mickey looks at me and sees I'm not joking. This love thing sucks and I'm tired of crying about it. It takes up way too much energy and I don't have any to spare and neither does she.

"Speak for yourself. I want the whole thing, and being in good with Nigel's parents is the only way I'm going to get it." The women in line turn around and look at Mickey like she's speaking over a loud speaker. She's adamant about her position, but not any louder than usual.

"But you already know Mr. and Mrs. Esop ain't going for it and probably never will." I look down and eye the few bags I have for my stuff and Rahima's outfit. I didn't get much, but it's enough to get me through the winter, especially with my new jacket to keep me warm.

"I'm working on that. Besides, once the baby's here they won't be able to resist their granddaughter." I look at Mickey and now realize she's in serious denial. Nigel's parents will never accept her as a part of their family, especially not the part that marries their NFL-hopeful son. I love my girl but she has to realize that everyone doesn't feel the same way about us Compton girls. She's considered fine around our hood, with her large bamboo earrings, curved acrylic nails, and ghetto-fabulous attire. But for Nigel's parents, Mickey's their worst nightmare come true, and they're not going to claim Mickey or her baby without a fight.

"Mickey, I don't think it's going to get any better," I say, moving in line right along with her. For a Wednesday evening, the crowd is out in full force and I'm tired of dealing with the public. All I want is to get back to my mom's and pass out on the couch while watching reruns of *Martin*.

"Watch and see. We're going to be one big happy family. Nigel and I want to be together and raise our baby up the right way." She takes her purchases to the next available register and pulls out her cash. Now she's getting an allowance from both her man and Nigel until her man finds out about her and Nigel running around. It must be nice, but the gravy train's going to end sooner than later and Mickey needs to wake up before it's too late. I hand my single purchase and the remainder of my shopping cash to the second cashier. Damn, money goes fast.

"Well, if I were you and Nigel, I'd find another way to get what I want, plain and simple. You need to get a job and keep it moving if being together is what y'all really want. Why do you need someone else's approval to get it done?"

"Because, Jayd, this shit's going to be hard without family and I can't do it alone." One of the elder white ladies behind the counter looks over her thin-framed glasses at Mickey, sizing her up just like Nigel's mom probably did the first time she saw her: a fast-ass girl looking for a dude with money. I'm not saying my girl's innocent, but she's not all bad, just a little misguided if you ask me.

"Well, you should've thought of that before, sis," I say as the cashiers finish the sales. Mickey hands the lady a one-hundred-dollar bill and the cashier promptly marks it with her special pen to make sure it's real. I wish it were that simple to tell real friends from the fake ones.

"Whatever, Jayd. We can't go back in time now," Mickey says, taking the small yellow bag from the cashier and leading the way out of the store. "We want to live together and be a family. Besides, they've got all of that room in their big-ass house and they haven't even finished the second floor. Nigel's bedroom is the only one up there so far. We can make it our own little love nest. They seemed so happy to meet me on Thanksgiving." That was before they found out she was knocked up by their baby boy.

"Mickey, do you live here on Earth with the rest of us?" I know she's got a right to her wishful thinking, but this girl is tripping if she thinks it's going to be another episode of *Reba.* "There's no way in hell you and your lovechild are going to be camping out at Nigel's house. At least not while his parents are living there."

"I don't see why not. I want to be Mrs. Nigel Esop and I'm going to live with my man no matter what his parents or mine have to say about it."

"Well, you're not dealing with the cards you've been dealt,

now are you, shawty?" I was trying to make Mickey smile but apparently her pregnancy hormones are in full swing because she's tearing up at my Mama-like advice.

"But I want to be with him. Why won't his parents accept me? I'm the mother of their grandchild whether they like it or not."

"Not," I say, shuddering at the thought of Mickey and Nigel walking down the aisle with his parents' blessing. "It'll be a cold day in hell before they accept a little ghetto girl from Compton marrying their all-star baby."

"Damn, Jayd, why you have to say it like that? I thought you was my girl?"

"I am your girl and I also know Nigel's parents, Mickey. There's a reason they moved out of Compton and to the west side. They wanted to get their precious children out of the hood we grew up in. Nigel and his sister have been pampered for as long as I've known him and it's not going to change anytime soon. I hate to be the one to break it down for you, but they see you as being more like Sandy than Tania, if you get my drift." She looks at me sternly, thinking about the comparison between Rah's baby-mama and Jeremy's. I guess that's enough of a reality check for her because her demeanor has now gone completely stiff.

"I won't accept that, Jayd. I can't. My daddy's expecting a ring on my finger before the baby gets here or he's not going to support us. This shit is screwed up. And I can't live in that house with all of those people for too much longer. I can't even get to the bathroom when I need to because of my brothers and sisters and that's not healthy for me or the baby." Mickey can be more dramatic than Nellie when she wants to. She's acting like she's in her third trimester when she's just ending the first.

"Those people are your family, Mickey, and you knew what you were doing when you did it." I look at a remorseful

Mickey and for the first time, I feel like she's being real with both of us.

"I can't bring my baby up like I was raised, Jayd. I won't." Now I see the calculative yet concerned Mickey hiding behind the street-girl persona. Mickey's had a plan all along to get up out of the hood and, more importantly, out of her house. My mom did the same thing and in both scenarios the ending's not a good one.

"I know, Mickey, I know." I understand why Mickey's scared, but she made this mess and now she's got to clean it up. Feeling winded, Mickey stops and leans up against the mall directory in the middle of the floor. From here we can see Nigel and Rah walking toward us from Macy's. It's about time they showed up.

"Look, Jayd. The truth is, Mrs. Esop's right about me. When my parents met my man they told me to have his baby if I was going to have one. And I tried for the longest to get pregnant by that fool." Mickey rubs her belly and I even think I see another tear in her eye. This is a record for her showing emotion. I think her hormones are making her feel more. "But I had two miscarriages in two years. I've never gotten this far before. That's why I know this is Nigel's baby. I got lucky this time, Jayd. Yes, I was hustling for a baby-daddy, but I wasn't counting on meeting Nigel. That was just pure luck."

"I hear you, Mickey. But I'm not the one you need to convince." I wish Nigel's folks were more understanding, but there's no sense praying for that miracle to occur. "And how does Nigel feel about you choosing to leave the main campus because you're pregnant? Does he know how the administration's treating you?"

"He doesn't know and I'm not telling him until I'm out, and I better not hear anything about you opening your big mouth, Judge Judy."

"I'm just saying you should fight for yours, and you

should definitely tell your man about it. This affects him too, Mickey."

"Jayd, we've been over this already and I'm done talking about it." I can tell Mickey doesn't really want to leave school but she feels powerless against our administration, unlike Tania, whose money made her teen pregnancy more tasteful, I assume. Her parents married her off the first chance they got but had she stayed, I'm sure the school wouldn't have asked her to check out like she did something wrong.

"Don't let someone else's hang-up keep you from getting what's rightfully yours, and staying in regular school is your right." As our boys get closer to where we're posted, Mickey's body language signals me to shut up but I'm not going to give up on my girl. I've already lost Nellie to the forces that be at South Bay High and I'm not about to lose Mickey, too.

"Can't you just cast some sort of spell or something to help me? It's Christmas for God's sake. We're supposed to be merry and shit." Mickey's still living in a fantasy world where Santa brings gifts down the chimney and true love lives happily ever after. That's not the love—or the holidays—that I know.

"Mickey, why did you think this was going to go over so easily? Did you really think they were going to be happy about their seventeen-year-old son, who's also up for football scholarships this year, becoming a father his senior year of high school? That doesn't sound good to them at all. Hell, it doesn't even sound good to me and I'm on your side."

"But it sounds perfect to me." I feel for my girl, but her naïveté is going to get her heart broken into tiny pieces if she doesn't snap out of it soon. "And you didn't answer my question, Jayd. Can you help me or not?" Even though she's asking—which makes it okay for me to try to help her—I know I can't help her out of this one.

"Mickey, this is way over my head. Besides, if you two really want to be together, you will. That's what family and love's all about: staying together no matter the obstacles. And my boy loves him some you, so I think you've got all the help you need in him." As Nigel approaches us I can see the look in his eyes. I look at Mickey and her smile is as big as his. I wish they could get the one gift they're both requesting this Christmas: to be together. But as with all gifts, even though we ask for them we don't necessarily get what we want.

"How's it going with you and Rah?" she asks as they approach us outside of the baby store, almost within earshot. I can't wait for Rahima to try on her new outfit. I hope I get to see her again soon, but with Sandy's unpredictable ass one never knows.

"It's going."

"Does he know you're still moonlighting with the white boy?" I give Mickey a cross look and ignore her snide question. She knows what's up with that.

"Hey baby," Nigel says, rubbing Mickey's belly before kissing her on the lips.

"Get a room," Rah says, and he's right. They can barely keep their hands off each other anytime they're together. I can see why his parents wouldn't want the two of them in their house on a daily basis.

"Don't hate," Nigel says, punching his boy in the arm.

"Damn, nigga. Watch the guns," Rah says, holding his right shoulder before reaching down to give me a bear hug. "Hey baby," he says, holding me tightly and rocking back and forth.

"Hey," I say, inhaling the soft scent of his Polo cologne and returning the love. "How was your day?"

"We made some money killing these fools on the court," Rah says, putting up his left hand for a high five from Nigel, who promptly obliges. "They didn't stand a chance, just like the mall didn't have a prayer against you two. How was shopping, ladies?"

"It was good," Mickey says, excitedly opening her bags to show off the baby clothes. "Look what I got our little princess."

"Wait a minute. We already have a baby girl in the crew. We're expecting a little homie," Nigel says. Rah smiles down at me and I return the gesture.

"Well, that'll have to wait until the next one comes along because this baby is definitely a girl. Now, look at your daughter's clothes." As they admire the expensive wardrobe for their unborn child, Rah and I shake our heads at the sight. I wish they could be together because they sure do love the idea of being one big happy family.

"Jayd, we have to get to the cell phone place before they close." Rah looks at his watch and starts to walk away from the happy couple, pulling me along with him. "And I also made you an appointment to change the registration on your car for tomorrow afternoon, since they won't be open because of the holiday on Friday. Is that cool with you?" Rah's been on it lately. If he keeps it up, I might get spoiled by all of this attention.

"Yeah, that sounds cool. How's Rahima?"

"Missing you, just like me," he says, bending down to kiss me on the neck.

"Get a room," Nigel yells at us, returning the love. Rah looks up at his boy and smiles. "We'll catch y'all later. My girls are hungry."

"Bye Jayd, and remember our conversation. There will be a quiz later," Mickey says, allowing Nigel to take the bags from her and lead her toward the food court.

"Bye y'all," I say. Which part of our conversation she's referring to I'm not really sure, because we covered a lot of ground this afternoon, but I'll worry about that later. Maybe she'll be one of the first calls I make on my new cell once it's programmed.

"So, you ready to give up on your raggedy cell?" I know Rah's only joking, but it still hurts. I'm attached to my first cell, even if it is on its last leg.

"Hey, this phone has served me well. But yes, I'm ready to upgrade," I say, taking out my new pink Razor cell, ready to switch. I turn the power on and wait for it to boot up. I only have two pictures on the phone. I saved the one Rah took of Rahima and me as the wallpaper background, so it pops up instantly. Rah looks over my shoulder and smiles.

"Yeah, now you can send me pics of you when I need to feel good." Rah takes my hand in his and escorts me toward the cell-phone booth downstairs. "And I'll send you some just in case you forget what a brother looks like at that white-ass school of yours."

"Whatever, Rah." I know that was a loaded statement about Jeremy, but I'm not going there with him today. Jeremy wants to come by tonight and I haven't told Rah yet, but now that I'm driving myself I don't have to explain anything to anyone. When I'm ready to leave, I just do, and that is more valuable to me than anything money can buy. "I can never forget that face," I say, reaching up to squeeze his chiseled cheek. Other people riding the escalators look at us and smile. We do make a cute couple from the outside looking in.

"You want to grab something to eat afterwards? I got to get my hustle on tonight, but we can kick it for a minute."

"Oh, I already have plans," I say as we get ready to step off the escalator. Once relaxed and smiling, now those same cheekbones are flexed and stressed. I better reroute some of his emotion by changing the subject, and fast. "Which hustle are we working on tonight?"

"My music. And what plans do you already have?" Damn, I guess my diversions need some work because he's still hot on my trail. I take the first step off and he's right behind me.

"Rah, we're having a pleasant evening. Let's just keep it like this, please." Rah stops walking, looks down at me, and takes a deep breath like he's about to give the speech of a lifetime. Before saying a thing, he notices my new North Face jacket for the first time and touches it gently. I know what he's thinking: How could I afford such an expensive jacket?

"If that fool didn't have money would you still be dealing with him?" I look back up at Rah, shocked at his question. Who does he think he's talking to, Mickey?

"Rah, now I know you know me better than that," I say, walking toward the cell-phone booth alone. Rah hasn't moved from his spot. He'd better come on. This is no time to show his ass and act a fool in the mall.

"I thought I did. But ever since this white boy came along you've changed."

"He has a name and I know you know what it is. When Jeremy refers to you he doesn't say 'that black boy' so show him the same respect," I say over my shoulder while Rah quickens his pace to catch up.

"He'd better not if he knows what's good for him." I stop in my tracks and look back at my long-time friend. Jealousy's never been a good look on him.

"Quit being such a baby. I can have other plans if I want to, just like you're free to still talk to Trish, or have you conveniently forgotten about the fact she still calls you every day?" Choosing to leave the question in the air, Rah and I continue to walk in silence.

When we reach the cell-phone store the line is out the door. I guess everyone got in on the holiday upgrade special. Rah stands outside while I get in line, looking torn between where he's standing and where I'm going. This wouldn't be the first time we've parted ways after a disagreement and it won't be the last, I'm sure.

"I'm only doing this because I'm a man of my word. Anything else you need, get your boy toy to get it for you." Rah takes his worn leather wallet out of his back pocket and opens it. He pulls out a one-hundred-dollar bill, hands it to me, and walks away from me. Damn, I know he's mad, but that was low.

"Rah, it's not that serious," I call after him. Why does everything have to be so difficult? I'll just have to call him after I'm done here.

I'm still not comfortable driving around in my little hoopty, especially since it has a tendency to overheat just like its caretaker, Rah. Rah hasn't spoken to me since he left me alone at the mall yesterday and he's not returning my calls. My car was tripping this morning when I drove it to work, but it seems to be okay now that I'm cruising around the beach. I told my dad about it and he says he'll take a look at it next time I come by. He just wants to make sure I drive the car that he bought me using the license he paid for me to get. Mama was right: the only reason my daddy helped me was to show off to his family, and I'm glad my mom's not rubbing it in my face anymore. As long as I get to roll when I want and where I want, it's all good to me.

After working all day and spending the evening at the mall with Mickey yesterday, I decide to chill by myself this afternoon, in Redondo Beach to start and then drive right on through the neighboring beach cities just to see if I can make it to and from without getting lost. As long as I stay on the main streets I'm good.

As I drive through the streets of Redondo, I notice all of the pretty lights on the big, beautiful houses are slowly coming down, some families ridding themselves of the holiday sooner than others. I know everyone has worries, but I just don't think the people living in these homes have the same stress as we do in our neck of the woods. All I ever think about is ways to hustle more money—legally. Most of the people I know just want money, damn the law, and at times I feel them. But Mama would kill me if I ever did anything illegal.

"Jayd, is that you?" Matt says from his SUV stopped at the red light next to me.

"Yeah. What's up with you?"

"Just hanging. You got a car for Christmas, I see. Sweet." He's got a ride full of friends but none that I recognize from school or the beach. He also has a Great Dane in the front seat. I guess that's the dog he's always talking about like it's his little brother. White folks and their animals.

"I'm glad you think so," I say, looking at the temperature gauge rise in my little car. I guess I'd better get back to Compton before it hits red. I need to let her rest if I want to make it back to my mom's tomorrow, and I need to. So far I have five heads lined up for the weekend and if I'm on my game I can fit a few more in before Sunday. I also need to make it to Netta's on Saturday and talk to her about my new work schedule now that I have my own wheels.

"Hey, we all have to start somewhere, girl. I'm happy for you. Your own wheels are the first step to independence. See you Monday," Matt says, speeding off into the sunset and reminding me of our return to Drama High next week. At least I can sleep in for a change, now that I don't have to wake up early for my usual three bus rides. I pass by a few of the bus stops on my route and smile that I'm no longer one of the many folks standing on the corner waiting for the bus. Before I can get too lost in my good feeling, I smell smoke coming from somewhere and from the way people are pointing and staring at me, I'd say it's coming from my ride.

"Oh hell no," I say, pulling into the nearest gas station and turning off the engine. Where is Rah when I need him? Well, he must've smelled the fire because he's finally calling me back.

"What's up with you," Rah says groggily. It's almost six and this fool's just waking up. But that's how it is when he gets lost in his music.

"What's up is this piece of shit car my daddy gave me. I'm stuck on Manhattan Beach Boulevard. Can you come help a sistah out or are you still pissed at me?"

"Have you ever heard of quitting while you're ahead?" I've always been warned about my mouth being too sassy and I guess that was his way of telling me nicely to shut up. "I'm on my way."

"Thank you," I say.

"You're welcome." It'll take Rah a good forty-five minutes before he gets here with the New Year's Eve and after-work traffic well underway. I might as well leave my ride here and walk across the street to The Coffee Bean and Tea Leaf, my favorite coffee house. Jeremy and I come here often when we hang out by the beach, and I never get tired of the menu. I'd better call Mama and let her know I'm going to be a little late for our annual date.

"Hey, Mama. What's shaking?" I ask while making my way into the busy spot. The smell of coffee always perks me up.

"Nothing much, little one. What's up with you?"

"Well, my car overheated and I'm in Hermosa Beach waiting for Rah to come check it out, so I'll be there as soon as I can."

"What would you do without that boy on your side?" Mama asks. If I didn't know better I'd say she was referring to our spat at the mall, but I didn't tell her about that. Knowing Mama, she's probably referring to some future event that I don't know anything about.

"I don't know but I'm glad he's here now." And not just because he got me a new phone to chat on.

"Jayd, you go on home to your mother's house. These fools in the neighborhood have already started shooting off their guns to celebrate New Year's, and I don't want you caught in the crossfire. But stay close to your spirit book tonight and get some studying done. Focus on getting your blessings through doing work from your own hands. That's how you keep what you've gained."

"Are you sure? I'm close to Redondo Beach and it's the same distance from here to you or my mom. I know you don't want to be alone." And frankly, neither do I. But I'm not hanging out or partying like the rest of my friends will be doing. I'd rather spend a quiet night in, like we always have.

"Jayd, get back to your mom's. I'll be fine and will see you on Sunday. You're getting off early tomorrow at Netta's to get ready for school on Monday, right?"

"Yeah, but I'd much rather hustle. I need all of the money I can get."

"There are lots of things more important than money and one of them is rest. Without your health you won't get very far in life to spend that money you're working so hard for."

"I know, Mama, you're right." I watch another car pull up, as I anxiously wait for Rah's Acura to arrive on the scene.

"I'm always right. Now go on and get, and call me when you make it back," Mama says before hanging up the phone. I hate to leave Mama alone without another female to help ward off the masculine energy in that house, but I must follow Mama's directions first and foremost, no matter how I might feel about it.

Finally, after I'm almost finished with my large Vanilla Ice Blended, Rah pulls up, ready to save me. "Come on, girl, I've got plans tonight," Rah says through his open window. No hi or hello. I guess he is still pissed.

"Jayd," his little brother Kamal yells out from the backseat.

"What's up, little man? My car's across the street," I say, pointing toward my broke-down vehicle and giving Kamal a high five.

"Alright. I'll get her cooled off, then follow you back to your mom's crib. Here, you drive my car back," he says, pulling up next to my car and getting out. What would I do without Rah, indeed?

When we get back to Inglewood, all I want to do is shower and watch television, but I can't ring in the New Year with Rah still mad at me, and judging by his puppy-dog eyes, I'd say he feels the same way. My mom and Karl have already started their evening festivities off at his house, so it's just me and the television tonight. And as far as I'm concerned, this is all I need to have a good time.

"I'm sorry I left you yesterday, but you really hurt me." I open the front door, toss my jacket and purse on the couch and run to the bathroom. When I come back out, Rah's standing by the door, waiting for an apology from me that ain't coming. From what I can see, I didn't do anything wrong.

"How did I hurt you? By not always being available when you want me to be?"

"No, by accepting expensive gifts from that punk when you already know what he's all about." Rah's jawbone tightens and he looks like he wants to punch the wall. He needs to check himself—and now, before he goes too far.

"Yes, I do know what he's all about and it isn't money, no matter what you may think." I look at him and notice his eyes soften, but I can tell he's still vexed enough to do some damage. We need to drop the subject. I walk into the kitchen and check the cabinets for snacks, ready for my big night in. I grab a bag of popcorn.

"Jayd, it's New Year's Eve. You can't sit at home and watch

TV all night." Rah's always into festivities and I know he remembers what happened on New Year's several years ago, so
I don't understand why he's pressuring me. My uncle's murder is always on my mind this time of year.

"Watch me," I say, popping the popcorn in the skillet
while sprinkling sea salt on it. Rah watches me shake the
food in total disbelief of my nonchalant attitude. "You should
get going before Kamal gets impatient and starts honking
your horn."

"It's Jeremy. He's coming over, isn't he?" This brotha is too
much for me sometimes. Actually, Jeremy will be ringing in
the holiday with his brothers. They have a tradition that I'm
positive includes lots of alcohol and pot; not my cup of tea.
Besides, I've had enough of his family and their version of
the holiday spirit.

"Not that I know of. Rah, why are tripping? You know I
like to keep to myself on this holiday, especially since Mama's
usually in a mood, if you recall. I feel better staying home,
just in case she needs me." I glance at the selection of drinks
in the bare refrigerator and settle for lemonade. I haven't
been shopping since Monday and I'm almost out of food.

"Jayd, your uncle Donnie died five years ago. It's time for
a new tradition, don't you think?" Maybe he's right, but this
isn't the year to change shit up. It's a volatile time and I don't
want to rock the boat any more than it's already shaking. My
powers are getting stronger and so is my ability to make my
own money, which Mama says is where the real power lies.
The last thing I want to do is break tradition, which Netta
swears brings bad luck. She even attributes the fact that I re-
ceived a dress just like the one Maman had in our vision on
Christmas Eve, to some sort of karmic payback, and I tend to
believe her.

Déjà vu like that represents a definite glitch in the system
and, just like in one of my favorite movies, *The Matrix*, I'm

taking note and reacting accordingly, and that starts by staying my ass at home like Mama requested. She had three dreams involving me and violence, and I'm not ignoring the warnings.

"I feel like I need to stay my ass right there on that couch." I take a large, white bowl out of the cabinet and put the hot snack in it, ready to get my grub on. "There's a *Degrassi* marathon on The N tonight and you know that's my show." Rah looks at me and knows I'm not budging.

"Jayd, for real. We need to be together to bring in the New Year right."

"Well, I'm not exactly kicking you out." Rah follows me into the living room where I plop down on my couch/bed and settle in for the weekend. I grab the remote and turn to The N where *Clueless* is on before my marathon. "Perfect. I love this movie. I'm straight for the evening." Rah stands over me with his arms crossed over his chest, his hoodie hanging loosely over his sweats. He's adorable and almost irresistible when he really wants something, but I want peace even more than I want to hang with him this evening.

"Don't forget to make a wish at midnight," Rah says, bending down to kiss me on the forehead. I have a lot to wish for, including another car, since the one I have doesn't seem to be working out. Rah walks back toward the front door, ready to leave me to my evening in.

"I won't, and you do the same." Last year after Mama fell asleep, I talked on the phone with Mickey and Nellie until the sun came up. This year I'm going to include their reconciliation in my wish. With all that's going on—the good and the bad—I want to share it with both Mickey and Nellie. We need each other to get through the rest of the year. Why are my girls tripping when we need each other the most?

~ 7 ~
My Girls

"It's deep how you can be so shallow."

—GNARLS BARKLEY

After all of the shooting to ring in the New Year was over Friday night, I finally got some sleep, but not much. I have a long school week ahead of me and I still have a few heads to braid before I get back to Compton tonight. The last thing I need is to be sleep-deprived while doing someone's hair. I remember the last time I lost a lot of sleep after my uncle Donnie was murdered. I saw all kinds of shit that ain't normal and I never want to go there again.

"Girl, your braid sheen is off the chain. You should sell this stuff," Shawntrese says, spraying more on her fresh corn-rows. I'm glad her hair's finally growing strong enough to braid up and it looks good on her.

"I do," I say, looking at the half-empty bottle in her hand. I've been perfecting my braid products during my days at Netta's and it seems to be working. So far I have three stead-ies in my Lady J line of hair care: braid sheen, twist gel and scalp cream. I haven't shown Mama yet but I plan on unveil-ing my new creations Tuesday when we're together at Netta's. She's been helping me get it right. But I'm finally sat-isfied with the recipes and I think Mama will be very proud.

"Yeah, it does look good," Shawntrese's new boyfriend says, stepping into the hallway and poking his head through

the open door. I didn't know he was laid up over there. If I
did I would've closed and locked the door. She has the worst
taste in men and I don't want him up in my mom's crib.

"Yeah, Jayd's got that magic touch. You should let her
hook you up, Leroy. She's good at hooking up the brothas,
too."

"I'm sure she is," he says, eyeing me a little too closely for
my taste. And he's got a head full of hair that looks like it's
never seen shampoo or conditioner. I'll have to charge him
double to fix that mess.

"Down boy," Shawntrese says, checking her man. I know
this girl's got my back and won't let her man get too fresh
with me: at least one of my girls does. Mickey hasn't called
me back and I've been calling her since Friday. I guess she
and Nigel got caught up during the weekend, with his parents gone on a church retreat until today. Mickey didn't get
to chill with him for New Year's Eve, but they've no doubt
made up for it by now.

"What? I'm just saying if she could hook up that big head
of yours she can work miracles on my dome, ain't that right,
little miss pretty?" Leroy looks at me like the hungry dog he
appears to be and smiles.

"Who you calling big head?" Shawntrese asks, slapping
him on his massive chest. This brother looks like he just got
out of the pen yesterday, as swole as his muscles are. What's
up with my girls and these thug dudes, I just don't know.

"Nah baby, I didn't mean it like that," he says, running
from her attack. I hate to side against Shawntrese but he is
right; she does have a big head in comparison to her petite,
boyish body. She's cute in an athletic sort of way. Shawntrese
has very small hips and her breasts are almost nonexistent.
But, she's got a behind as hard as a rock and that keeps the
brothas on her jock, not to mention her bright smile.

"Look, if you want to get hooked up then let's get to it. I

have to leave soon and it's going to take awhile to get all that in check." They stop playing around and get serious.

"Alright, Miss Lady. You serious about your time and I like that," Leroy says, sitting down at the dining room table with Shawntrese following suit and landing on his lap. "How much you charge?" I run my fingers through his filthy scalp and close my eyes. I read about Maman Marie doing the same thing with her clients and have taken on the practice myself, and it seems to be working to my advantage. No two heads are the same and no two clients get the same treatment, as Netta would say.

"Twenty an hour and it's going to take me about two hours to do your hair. Don't move yet," I say, putting my right hand on his shoulder while my left continues making the trek through his thick afro. I can see approximately twenty braids in his head, thin parts and coming back at an angle with the two sides meeting in the middle. I can't explain it, but seeing the braids or style before I start helps it come to life while I'm doing it.

"That's cool. Do your thang," Leroy says while my eyes are still closed. I can feel my girl looking up at me from her man's lap. I know she's wondering what the hell I'm doing to his head.

"Jayd, what the hell are you doing?" she asks, taking the thought right out of my mind.

"I'm working," I answer, still in my vision. "I can tell he wears a bandana most days by his smooth edges, but that's going to have to stop if he wants his receding hairline to stop growing," I say, opening my eyes and selecting a comb from the hair tools spread across the dining room table. I'll have to replace my mom's permanent place settings, and the vase of flowers Karl keeps full for her, before I leave. I also need to vacuum because I have hair all over the place from the various clients I've worked on this weekend.

"What is she, some sort of psychic or something?" If he only knew the half of it. I've had more visions doing folks' hair these past two weeks than ever before. Netta says it's because of the exchange in ashe going on, and Mama insists that I learn how to rid myself of it before it damages me. According to the spirit book, every Williams woman must define her generation and, more importantly, come up with her own signature style, which includes a cleansing for self-preservation. I think I've got the style down, it's just the cleansing that's keeping me guessing.

"Nah, she's just strange, but she's my girl though." Shawntrese has always known I'm a little different and has never minded.

"Okay, let's take it to the sink, Buckwheat," I say, draping a clean towel around Leroy's shoulders before Shawntrese moves to the couch to watch television. Before I can get too involved in my new client's scalp treatment, my phone rings. Finally, my girl calls me back.

"Jayd's House of Hair," I say, throwing Mickey off a little.

"Jayd, stop playing before you get hung up on." She sounds like she's in a good mood. I hope that means she told Nigel about the school bullying her into submission and he talked some sense into her.

"That's a good title for your business. You should copyright that," Shawntrese says, adding her two cents. Now that she's almost finished with her Associate's Degree in business, I guess she's going to be all up in everyone's business even more than she already is. At least now she'll have a certificate to do it.

"Anyways girl, what's up with you?" I ask, propping the phone between my shoulder and ear so I can talk and work at the same time. I then take my comb and start to part and scratch the dandruff out of this brother's scalp. He's bent over the sink and I intend on all of these flakes going down the drain. Damn, now I'm going to have to disinfect my mom's sink before I leave, too.

"We're good, me and my family. How was your weekend?"

"It was cool, just hustling. You know how I do it." After I finish scratching Leroy's head, I take the peppermint and lavender shampoo Mama makes especially for dandruff-ridden clients and pour it all over his head. The effervescent scent fills the small kitchen, instantly calming my nerves. And from the look of it, the scent is having the same effect on Leroy.

"Yeah, not at all," Mickey says, making herself laugh.

"Did you call to harass me or what?" I gently massage the liquid into Leroy's scalp, making sure to cover every inch of hair and skin. I then scrub more forcefully, ridding him of his past hair products. After using Mama and Netta's line of hair products, as well as my own, I can never go back to store-bought stuff again.

"Where'd you get that shampoo? I can smell it all over the house," Shawntrese says, coming into the kitchen and making it too close for comfort. I've got to get off the phone and focus on getting my work done so I can relax. Otherwise, I'm not going to have a good morning getting ready for school tomorrow.

"My grandmother makes it." I can hear Mickey's heavy breathing over the phone. She doesn't like being ignored by anyone.

"Well, I can see you're busy. What, do you have a fan club now?" Mickey can be real funny when she wants to be and she's cracking herself up this afternoon.

"No, just satisfied customers."

"Damn straight," Shawntrese says, smacking her man on the behind before returning to the living room. Leroy barely moves, he's so relaxed. That means I'm doing my job.

"You should let me hook you up," I say. Mickey's silence speaks volumes.

"Jayd, I don't think so." Enough said. I don't want to get offended by my last homegirl at South Bay. Besides, I have enough of her ashe to shake off as it is. "I have a steady stylist and we go way back." Yeah, and so do her highlights and extensions. But Mickey's my girl and if she likes it, I love it.

"Alright then. Let me call you back when I get to Compton later on. I should be done here in a couple of hours."

"Okay then. Holla," Mickey says before hanging up. I can tell she didn't want anything too serious, but it is the first day back tomorrow and we have to catch up before we get to school in the morning.

"Jayd, do you give out samples? I need to slang some of this around the hood," Leroy says as I rinse his hair, ready for a second wash. If he likes this then he's going to love the coco-mango conditioner I've got for him next. I'll use my own products to braid him up with.

"I never thought about it but that's a good idea." Why not pimp my products like Mama does? It'll be more money in my pocket and a way to help out folks, with natural options for their crowns. I'll probably even get some more clientele out of it. Right now, I just need to finish this one client and get moving. I want to make sure I have any and all work that may be due in my classes, including my government paper. Hopefully Mrs. Peterson won't be that mean, but I know her better than that.

My car didn't overheat on the way back to Mama's and for that I am truly grateful. Rah has mad skills when it comes to cars and music production. I just wish he were better at managing his personal life. We kicked it this weekend, but without his daughter. I can't help but miss Rahima when she's not around. I hope his court case at the end of the week ends favorably. Otherwise, I can count on Rah being in a bad mood eternally, and that's not good for anyone. I also hope it ends with his little girl in his home for her own sake. Even if Rah is still in school and slanging, I know he'll do right by his child, and his grandparents will help in any way they can. Rahima's sweet disposition and loveable spirit are fragile and she needs to be raised in the right hands, and those hands unfortunately don't belong to her mother.

Speaking of unfit mothers, I notice Misty's mother's car parked outside of Esmeralda's house. I wonder if Misty's over there too. I just hope we all keep our distance from each other, mainly Esmeralda from me. That lady works my nerves even when she's not around. Although I can't see Esmeralda I know she sees me, and that's not a good feeling. I can see why my mom moved out the first chance she got. Anonymity isn't an option on our block.

I park my car right in front of the house so I can keep an eye on it. I'm not really worried about anyone jacking the car, especially considering the dilapidated state it's in. But I still don't want anyone breaking into my shit. Glass costs money just like anything else and I'm not spending any more of my hard-earned cash on this thing .

Before I can get through the back door good my phone rings. Damn, Mickey's on my jock this evening. Whatever she wants to talk about must be important.

"Yes Mickey," I say, stepping over a sleeping Lexi and through the kitchen door. I put down my garbage bag full of dirty clothes, set my weekend bag and backpack on the floor, and take a seat at the table. I guess I'll be doing laundry tonight if no one else is in the garage using the machines already. It's Jay's first day back to school tomorrow too, and I know he has mad clothes to wash just like I do. Mama's out with Netta this evening so I'll have the bedroom all to myself once I make it back there.

"I've had it with that bitch," Mickey says, waking my tired ass right up.

"Which bitch?" It's a fair question considering how many girls have earned that title in Mickey's book. I'm sure even I get called the occasional bitch when the mood suits her.

"The original bitch. Your girl Nellie." Here we go. I roll my eyes and prepare to hear my girl vent. I know she misses our third musketeer just as much as I do, but Mickey will never admit it. She'd rather just talk shit about her.

"Nellie's no more my girl than she is yours, if you recall correctly." I reach for my backpack and take out my multiple school folders. I might as well check my schoolwork while I'm sitting here.

"Whatever. I saw her at the mall earlier and she and her little white friends were talking shit about me, I just know it."

"Haven't you had enough of the mall? You've been to a different one almost every day we've been on vacation."

"That's not the point, Jayd," Mickey says, now completely irritated. Getting through this pregnancy is proving to be anything but easy. "She's got her nerve and then some, trying to talk shit without coming right up to me and saying something. She's forgotten who she's messing with." I hope Mickey never finds out that Nellie ratted out her, Nigel, and myself so she could be in Laura's clique. As mad as I am at Nellie right now, I still don't want to see her get her ass beat by Mickey. Just the thought of it makes me cringe. Fighting an enemy usually isn't as personal as going at it with a homegirl. And, as tight as they once were, Mickey's liable to kill Nellie for what she's done.

"Mickey, you can't let what you think she said bother you. Stress isn't good for you or the baby." I look over my English folder and everything looks like it's in good order. Hopefully the mandatory AP meetings won't resume after the new semester begins in a few weeks. I can't take much more of Mrs. Bennett, especially after being forced to deal with her in rehearsal during the last month of drama class. I'm not looking forward to seeing her tomorrow, but I can't run from my destiny. If she finds proof that I forged Mickey's absences then so be it. I'll just have to deal with the consequences and I might have to kick Nellie's ass myself for squealing to the administration.

"I'm just saying, if that trick says one word to me I'm slapping her in the face, hard," Mickey says through my new cell. I love that I can put my phone on speaker, but I don't love the words that are coming through it. Life was so much easier when Nellie and Mickey were friends. Now there's just not enough balance in my life, and my girls are making me tired.

"Mickey, have you ever heard of thinking positively about the situation? You have enough fighting on your plate." I open my government folder and take out my paper on Queen Califia. Five pages don't do my great ancestor any justice, but it'll have to do for Mrs. Peterson's class. I couldn't find valid proof that she existed, but there's enough oral history and art to make a good case, so even Mrs. Peterson won't be able to deny Califia's contribution to California history.

"Who are you talking about?"

"It's not a who, it's a what," I say, thinking about my many battles with the administration at South Bay High. "You're going to have to plead your case to the powers that be at our lovely high school."

"I ain't pleading a damn thing to anyone. I'd rather go to the continuation school than fight with them fools, and for what? School is school, and we'll still see each other. And you know they can't keep me from seeing Nigel on a regular basis, so I'm straight."

"Mickey, you can't be serious?"

"How come I can't? I've got better things to do than fight with those fools. And the letter says my parents would have to come up there and sign some affidavit, and you know they're not going to be bothered with all of that." I know how she feels in that regard. Mama wouldn't waste her time, and my mom can't be bothered with missing a day from work to deal with my school.

"Mickey, this shit is serious. They could keep you out through senior year if you don't contest the decision now. Did you know that for as long as your baby's in diapers they can keep you out of a regular school environment if you let them? I read over the school's guidelines and bylaws yesterday and it says that you have the right to a hearing. If your parents cannot be present another adult can act on their behalf."

"Jayd, you're taking this way too seriously. It's not a big deal."

"And you're not taking it seriously enough. Don't you care about your education?" I can hear Mickey breathing through the phone but I'm not sure she's listening to a word I'm saying.

"Yeah, but not that much. I'm just not into school like you are."

"Mickey, why are you at South Bay if you don't care about school?"

"Because I got sick of fighting every day at Centennial High. And my daddy wanted to distance me from my man, not that it helped much."

"Mickey, you have the opportunity to set a precedent for other girls in your predicament. Don't let them bully you into submission."

"No one's bullying me, Jayd. You sound like an after-school special, with all of your big words and shit. Damn, once you get on your soapbox you don't get off, do you?"

"Not when it's something like this. I could ask Ms. Toni to step in for your parents, if you like. Or maybe Mr. Adewale would be willing to play your daddy," I say, trying to make a joke, but Mickey's deep sigh tells me she's not finding me humorous at all.

"Jayd, there are times to fight and times to just keep it moving, you feel me? I'm going to focus on me and Nigel and our baby being a family, which means keeping quiet for his sake as well. I don't want to make trouble for him at school. He's already dealing with his family. So please, just shut up about it. It's not your problem. See you in the morning." Mickey hangs up the phone, taking the last word with her. I can't stand it when she does that.

I look over my papers and everything seems to be in order. Besides, I can't concentrate on this stuff when my girl is in so much trouble. I might as well pick out my school clothes and take an early bath. I need to be in a good mood for tomorrow. Seeing all of my friends, enemies, and the people in between will drain me, and I don't want to be unprepared for the battle.

When I arrived at school this morning I was hella early because I didn't know exactly how long it would take me to get here. I made it in thirty minutes, and that's without traffic. Maybe I can leave a little later tomorrow and sleep in even longer. That alone would be worth driving this deathtrap around. I parked in the parking space closest to the front entrance, and Mickey's the first of my crew to arrive even if she wants to be here the least.

"That was the shortest two weeks ever," Mickey says, rubbing her growing belly. She finally broke down and bought some maternity clothes and she looks cute in them, too. "We need at least a month from this place."

"I agree," Chance says, scanning the parking lot for his girl. But instead of catching Nellie, we see Misty. Damn, I don't want to see her today. I haven't run into her since I saw her at Esmeralda's house on Christmas, and it's been a nice break. Mickey sees Nigel pull up in the other lot and goes to meet her man.

"Hey Jayd," KJ says. He, Money, Del, and Misty all look like they went shopping at the Swap Meet over the holiday, sporting new gear right down to their socks. "How was your holiday?" Misty looks less than happy that her supposed man's making small talk with me and honestly, I can feel her on this one.

"It was cool," I say, not returning the inquiry. His boys look at each other then at my ride and start to snicker. Oh, I see. They came over here to clown.

"Yeah, I can see that. Nice ride."

"I know you ain't talking with your piece of shit over there," I say, nodding toward his old Toyota.

"Yeah, but you see my new twenty-twos and I got new speakers in the trunk. You look like you need, well, another car." His boys and Misty get a good laugh out of KJ's insults but then Chance responds. He takes his keychain out of his jeans pocket and presses a button on his alarm, starting his classic Nova. The speakers immediately start to throb. Lil Wayne never sounded so good.

"Do they sound like that?" Chance asks KJ, who now looks completely deflated. "Didn't think so." I hate that the brothas had to get punked by a white boy, but that's what they get for trying to clown my ride.

"Whatever, man," Del says, coming to his boy's defense. KJ looks at Chance and knows he can't say shit. "Rich white boys can get anything they want. It still doesn't make your car look any better, Jayd." Why is Del hating on me so hard right now? Is he that jealous of someone else getting a car while he's still buying a backup bus pass?

"And what do you have? You and your boy here are just some scrubs lucky enough to get a ride with your boy right here," I say, tired of them. "Y'all are trifling and everyone

knows it." Misty looks at me with narrow eyes like she wants
to do something to me she knows she doesn't have the
power to do. I wish she would try to put something on me.
I'd give her a run for her money plus some.

"So defensive this morning, aren't we, Jayd?" Misty asks,
stepping in front of her boys, if I can even call them that. I
must say this is the longest KJ's ever kept a girl around.
Maybe she's paying him with more than her obvious assets.

"Not at all. You should tell your boyfriend to get a new
hobby. Antagonizing me is your sport, isn't it?" Chance
laughs at my sarcasm and nods his head toward campus, indicating it's time to roll, and I'm right behind him. Before we
can escape the scene of broken egos, Misty steps in front of
me, forcing me to look down at her short ass. I know I can't
really talk with my five-foot self, but next to Misty I feel like
Shaquille O'Neal.

"So, I didn't see you around for New Year's. You too good
to hang out in Compton with the rest of us?" Why would
Misty be checking for me when we're not girls anymore? I
know she's nosy, but damn. This is borderline stalking.

"Since when do you care where am I or what I do?" Between hanging with KJ and being under Esmeralda's wing,
she's really gone off the deep end. Before Misty can answer, I
notice my real girl and homeboy coming our way.

"Hey, Jayd," Mickey says, walking up the lot with Nigel
right by her side. They must have come in through the back
entrance.

"Hey, y'all," I say, not taking my eyes off of Misty, who's
waiting for an answer from me that's never coming.

"What's going on here?" Nigel asks, noticing the tense vibe
between me, Misty, KJ, and his boys. All of the other students
are happy to see each other and for the most part they seem
happy to be back at school. But of course, the black folks

have to bring the drama back to school with them. What the hell? I'm tired of being a part of this shit.

"Nothing. Nothing at all," I say, defusing the situation before we all get carried away. I'm still curious as to why Misty would miss me being at Mama's house on New Year's, but I'll let it slide for now. "We'd better get to class before the bell rings."

"Yeah, let's," Mickey says, stepping up next to me, which instantly causes Misty to stand down. Ever since Mickey busted her out for catching gonorrhea from KJ, Misty avoids her at all costs. KJ and his boys retreat right behind her and I'm grateful for the space.

"I wonder what's keeping Nellie," Chance says as we walk toward campus, causing Mickey to suck her teeth loudly. "I guess I'll have to catch her at break," he says as the first bell rings. It's time for all of us to face the rest of our inevitable first day back. Hopefully it'll get better as the day progresses.

My first two classes went by without incident. Mr. Donald wasn't even there for Spanish, and in English class Mrs. Malone wanted us to write an essay reflecting on what it means to come into a New Year. Personally, I'm just glad to be alive and working hard, and that's pretty much what I wrote down.

I'm not looking forward to third period at all. Why the nutrition break is only twenty minutes long baffles the hell out of me. It should be at least a half hour, not that there's ever enough time to get ready for Mrs. Peterson.

"Jayd, wait up," Chance says, catching up to me on my way into the main hall. I need to switch out my books for my next two classes. I also want to avoid Misty and Nellie for the rest of the day, if possible. I feel like if I can avoid them I can avoid drama, but no such luck. Nellie, Laura, and the rest of the ASB bitches are lined up outside of the ASB room and the rest of the clique's probably inside holding Ms. Toni hostage with their boring holiday stories. I'll have to catch up with my favorite teacher later in the week, preferably when these broads won't be around.

"What's up, Chance? You see your diva's straight ahead, don't you?" Even if Nellie's not talking to me, she can't keep me and Chance from being friends, although I know she's trying hard to tempt Chance to the dark side.

"Yeah, I know," he says, waving to Nellie, who gives him an evil look in return. "Listen, I want to talk to you about your car," he says, stepping in front of me and walking backwards. Nellie notices the change and tenses up at the sight.

"What about it?" I ask, stopping at my locker and entering the combination.

"We can hook it up, if you let us. Me and Jeremy love projects. Well, not Jeremy so much because he'd rather surf than work on a car, but if it's your car I'm sure he'd make an exception." I know Chance means well, but having my little hoopty be their rags-to-riches project is not my idea of a blessing.

"That's really sweet of you, Chance, but I don't think that's such a good idea," I say, watching Nellie and her new girls approach us from over his shoulder.

"Why not? You see how sweet my ride is? I can do the same for you, girl."

"But you don't have to. Besides, what would your girl say if she knew you pimped my ride?" Chance turns around to an angry Nellie looking up at him. I shut my locker door and begin to walk toward my government class only to see Mickey speed-walking our way, with Misty not too far behind her. Please don't tell me this trick let it slip that we have Nellie to thank for the administration finding out about Mickey's forged absence letters. Mickey already wants to kill Misty, and now that she's leaving the school there's nothing stopping her.

I turn around to warn Chance and his girl of the impending collision, only to see that Nellie has something of her own to say. "Jayd, can't you find your own man to play with? Oh, that's right, you don't have one at the moment."

"You know I would warn you that Mickey's on her way over, but I'll just let her at you instead." Nellie looks past us and sees Mickey, who's now breathing over my shoulder.

"Guess what I heard?" Mickey says, stepping in front of me and looking eye-to-eye with Nellie, who's shaking behind her brave stance. Laura and the rest of their crew look on, waiting for the next move like the rest of us. Students are slowly making their way back into the large hall and all eyes are pulled to our small group.

"What did you hear?" Nellie asks, taking the bait. I must say I'm impressed with her newfound badass-ness, even if she is applying it in the wrong direction.

"I heard that a little birdie told on someone to get what she wanted. And then I heard that the little birdie got its ass kicked all over campus," Mickey says, reaching around me and pushing Nellie's shoulder with the tip of her long nail. If she's willing to break one of those claws I know she's one step away from taking the multiple gold earrings off of her ears in preparation for a fight.

"Mickey, take a Pamprin. Oh, that's right. Your bitchiness is caused from not having a period to worry about these days," Nellie says as Laura looks on, proud of her protégé. They both look down at Mickey's growing belly like it's something to be ashamed of. I don't like anyone sending negative ashe to an innocent baby.

"Okay you two, let's just calm down," I say, trying to appease the situation. I don't know why I care about these two remaining friends, but I do, and I can't stand giving our enemies the satisfaction of seeing our crew in shambles. It used to be the three of us against the rest of these fools up here. But now that one of us has joined the fools, everything's off balance.

"Oh, Jayd. Always the martyr," Nellie says, mocking my intervention. "You know, we became BACs this Christmas. Maybe you two should try church. It works." Nellie hands me a flyer recruiting students for their after-school Born Again Christians club. I thought schools were the one place all religions were forbidden and that's just fine by me. There's never a flyer going around for my religion. Maybe I should start my own club.

"You can't be serious," Chance says, snatching up the flyer and laughing. "Laura, you're the biggest skank I know," Chance says, much to Nellie's disapproval.

"Whatever," Laura replies. There's nothing else the girl can say, because she knows he's telling the truth and so do I. Mickey looks at Nellie like she's a stranger, but I'm not willing to let this go so easily, even if the ringing bell says that I have to.

"You don't even like religion," I yell at Nellie as the hall becomes louder with the growing crowd.

"Well, my soul needs saving after dealing with heathens like you and Mickey. You've both been a bad influence on me and I needed something new."

"No, what you need is a good ass whipping and I'll gladly give you one," Mickey says before taking off the first earring, and I don't know if I can stop her, even if she is pregnant. Misty's still looking on, watching us go back and forth like a cat watching a tennis match. She really needs to get a life and I need to focus on saving my girls from ripping each other apart.

"Nellie, after all they did to you: putting up naked pictures of you on the Internet, making you anorexic, and then planting a rotten apple for you to eat, I can't believe you still want to hang with them. But you know what? You go right ahead. Me and Mickey will keep it moving without you, and we'll be here when you wise up, as always."

"Speak for yourself," Mickey says, rubbing her belly. "I've got a baby to think about now. All of her little shit don't matter to me anymore." Mickey calms down and puts her earring back on, ready to walk to third period. "You can hang with whoever you want to. I'm done with your trifling ass." Nellie looks sincerely hurt by Mickey's words. For a split second she has my sympathy.

"You know you're going straight to hell for your sins, right Mickey? I'll be here when you're ready to repent. Bye bye," Nellie says, walking back into the ASB right behind the rest of her clique, Chance behind her. She's really tripping this time. And, unlike last time, I'm going to let her fall flat on her face and I'm going to move out of the way 'cause she's crashing into unknown territory for me and I don't want to get hurt in the crossfire.

"Mickey, are you okay?" I ask, watching her pace back and forth. I know it took a lot of restraint for her not to kill Nellie and I'm proud of my girl. She's so hot I feel like she's going to explode, and that can't be good for the baby.

"I have to check in with the administration at lunch about transferring to the continuation school. I'll catch you after school, Jayd."

"Mickey, I'm telling you, don't let them derail you like this. It's not a good move."

"Maybe not, but it's my move to make. Later," she says, waddling off toward her class and me to mine. I'd better get a move on because the last thing I want to do is be late for third period.

I make it to class on time, but barely.

"Thank you for joining us today, Miss Jackson," Mrs. Peterson says from her desk. When Mr. A was here the last week before the break, I was hoping she'd be out permanently, but no such luck. This holiday season has sucked, through and through. No sense in it getting any better now that it's officially over.

"The bell is ringing as we speak. You can't mark me tardy for that," I say before putting down my backpack on my desk, which is next to Jeremy's empty one. I wonder if he forgot about school starting today? It is a nice, sunny, and windy day, making for the perfect surf. Perhaps he decided to take an extra day off before getting back on his grind. As I pull my chair out from under the desk, Mrs. Peterson waves her red pen in the air like a magic wand before continuing.

"Not so fast, Miss Jackson." The entire class laughs as she puts me on the spot, but for what I'm not sure. "As I announced a moment ago, the last person to arrive will be the first one to present their paper. You do have your paper ready, don't you?" Man, if she wasn't a teacher I'd take my earrings off right now and give her a run for her money. I'm already vexed about Nellie and Misty, not to mention Mickey leaving main campus in a couple of weeks. But now this heffa wants to put me on the spot my first day back after the winter break. What the hell?

"I'm ready." I get out my folder and take the five-page paper out, ready to present it, when Jeremy walks in right after the bell. Mrs. Peterson looks at me, pissed that I'm not the latest one and therefore not required to go first. But now that I'm up here, I might as well go ahead.

"Sorry I'm late," Jeremy says, looking like he just rolled out of bed.

"That's okay, Mr. Weiner. Please get ready to grace us with your report. Miss Jackson, you can take your seat."

"Actually, I'd like to go ahead since I'm already up here." Mrs. Peterson looks at me and shakes her head.

"Fine, Jayd. Go ahead. Mr. Weiner, you're next."

"Actually, I think we can go at the same time. Our leaders are kind of connected," he says, pulling out his paper. "I changed my topic to the ruler Cortes, the one who named California after his love, Califia." This dude is tripping big time if he thinks Mrs. Peterson's going to go for that. But before I can contest, the vision of Maman's white lover coming to the door to save her pops into my mind. Why is Jeremy always trying to save me like I need his help?

"I think I can handle this on my own," I say, smiling, but I really want to cuss him out for this. When did he make this change? As much as we saw each other over the break he didn't think to tell me? With friends like mine, I don't need any enemies. Too bad I've got both.

"This is a solo project, Mr. Weiner. You'll have to wait your turn. Miss Jackson, you may proceed." Jeremy reluctantly takes his seat and smiles at me like he's proud of his actions. Wait until I get to him at lunch. He won't know what hit him.

~ 8 ~
Money, Power, Respect

"Ladies is pimps too/
Go on brush your shoulders off."

—JAY Z

After class yesterday Jeremy left campus for the rest of the day. I never got to talk to him about his sudden change in topic for his report. We both ended up with good grades but it still doesn't excuse him for always trying to save me. Why can't Jeremy get it through his thick skull that he's not my daddy or my savior? I can save myself, or hasn't he noticed that by now? With my cupcakes I helped save his ass from going to jail, even if he doesn't believe it. Keeping him at school after he was busted selling weed was my first solo project.

Yesterday was so much excitement for me that I decided to come home right after school and study for my test with Netta and Mama, which is coming up soon. It would be too much like the right thing for them to tell me exactly when it's going to be. So, I'll just be prepared for whenever they're in the mood to spring it on me, even if it's today. After yesterday's surprise presentation in government, I'm reminded to expect anything at any time.

I throw the covers back and let the morning cold wake me up. Every morning I have to mentally prepare myself for the day ahead. I feel like I move from one world at home and into another one at school, and the shift isn't always smooth. But getting up a half hour later every morning, now that I can drive myself, should be helpful. Yesterday I made the mistake of going to school early and I ran into all sorts of drama. This morning I'll roll with the late crowd and pull up right as school begins.

"Good morning, sleeping stank breath," Bryan says. I sock him in the arm as he passes me up in the hallway. "Such violence so early. You're already going to be late if you don't quit playing."

"Ain't nobody gon' be late," I say, pushing him aside to get into the room he shares with my grandfather and cousin Jay. I'll be so glad when the day comes that I have my own room. Until then I'm stuck with storing my stuff in their closet.

"Oh, what are you going to do? Fly to Redondo Beach because you know you're about to miss your bus." I forget Bryan hasn't seen me since Christmas Eve because he's been shacking up at his girl's house for the holidays. He wasn't in when I got home from school last night, so maybe he's just coming up for air. He grabs his "Compton" baseball hat and puts it on over his neat braids. My work does last a long time, but his head is screaming for a new set of rows.

"You know my daddy bought me a car, right?" I say, making my way into the bathroom. I admit I'm a little embarrassed to drive my car. But as long as it keeps rolling, I'm a happy little black girl. Yesterday was my first day driving to school and it was pretty uneventful. I'm just glad it didn't break down at school. I would've never lived that down.

"Yeah? Does your daddy need a new son?" Bryan jokes. "I wish my daddy bought me a car."

"I did," Daddy says, stepping out of his bedroom, still half asleep. "It's not my fault you didn't take care of that van." Bryan looks at me like a little boy who's just been scolded for losing his bike. Daddy's a big man of few words: a dangerous combination, especially when he has the legal right to whip your ass.

"I was just playing, man," Bryan says, trying to clean it up. Daddy kisses me on the forehead and continues his trek toward the kitchen. Getting up later means more traffic and conversation that I don't have time for.

"If you're done being all up in my business now I need to get ready for school."

"Don't act like you didn't miss me, girl. I haven't seen you in over a week. And I didn't get to holla at you for New Year's like I usually do. I was in and out real quick, but I still checked for you."

"Yeah, Mama didn't want me out and I was running late that night. Did I miss anything?" I ask, separating my toiletries and spreading them across the small sink. I hang my long jean skirt and red shirt on the back of the bathroom door, ready to get dressed and get out.

"You know what's crazy is that I saw Misty on New Year's Eve go over to Esmeralda's and she looked like she didn't recognize me when I walked by. Maybe she was high or something," Bryan says. Misty has been looking a little strange lately but I just thought she was still recovering from her unfortunate bout with the clap.

"She's a trip. You know that," I say. Misty's one of the rare people I know who doesn't need any pharmaceutical help to bug out.

"Yeah, but she ain't that much of a trip. You should've seen her. Even Mama had to say something when she saw them go inside."

"Wait, Mama knew about it?" I wonder why she didn't mention this to me before. That would explain why Misty asked where I was for the holiday. I wonder what they were up to over there in that hellhole of a house, because I know it wasn't popping champagne and making happy wishes. Nothing about Esmeralda's creepy house says good times.

"M-hmm, and she went to the backhouse and stayed there until the next morning, or at least that's what Jay said when I came home the next day." Very interesting. Maybe that's why she didn't want me to come home on New Year's Eve. There was something going on she didn't want me to be around for. I wonder what? I'll have to check the spirit book when I get home and see if I can find any clues.

When I get to campus the cars are backed up down the same block I used to walk up every morning from the bus stop. There's something to be said about perspective, because from the inside looking out, I wish I were walking up the steep hill instead of waiting my turn to park. This is a waste of time, and if they don't move it up we're all going to be late for first period.

As I finally pull into the front parking lot, I can see Misty hanging up something on the bulletin board. It looks like a flyer for some sort of dance. Don't tell me she's volunteering for ASB now. Having a common target for hating sure does make for the strangest friends. I park in a spot far from the front gate we all have to go through to get to the main campus. Whether on foot or in a car, I still have to hustle to get to class on time. And after yesterday's falling out between Mickey and Nellie, I'm not really looking forward to today, even if we do get out early because of the usual Tuesday staff meeting.

"*Que pasa*, Jayd? You look a little down," Maggie says, walking toward the main hall without the rest of her crew. Usually you'd never see a member of El Barrio alone, but I guess every girl needs her space sometimes.

"Is it that obvious?" Maggie's the only female up here not tripping on me, I swear, and she never has.

"What's up, *chica*? You're not letting those girls of yours get to you, are you?"

"Of course I am. They're my girls."

"*Were*. They *were* your girls. Now they are just some chicks causing *muchas problemas in tu mundo*, no?" She's right. Nellie and Mickey have been causing major problems in my world and it's been turned upside down because of them both. They need to grow up and come to their senses before they end up on my bad side. Now that would be a strange world, where the three of us are enemies.

"Well, let's not count Mickey out. She's just dealing with a lot of pressure right now." Most of it caused by her own hands, but that goes without saying. "And I'm staying busy with work, so I'm trying to stay out of the mix as much as possible."

"Yeah, I heard about your mad hair skills. Want to hook me up?" Maggie says, smiling at me while twisting her long, curly brown hair. "Don't worry. Papi can give you a ride home. We all live that way too you know."

"Oh, I've got my own wheels now," I say, stopping in front of the main hall and putting my fingers through her hair like I do all of my clients. I can see two rows of tiny cornrows for Maggie, as opposed to the single row of partial braids she's rocking now. "Yeah, I'll hook you up one of these days."

"So it is true? You are turning this school into a beauty shop," Mrs. Bennett says. She and Mr. Adewale surprise us as they cross our path on their way to the main office. It sure is nice to see Mr. A this morning. I wish he had been here for my presentation of my paper on Queen Califia yesterday. I think he would have been pleasantly surprised.

"Actually, that's a good idea. We should have a beauty shop elective and Jayd could do her thang for everyone, including teachers," Maggie says, eyeing Mrs. Bennett's old-school haircut. Mr. Adewale clears his throat, trying not to laugh at Maggie's comment.

"Good morning, ladies," he says. Mrs. Bennett rolls her blues eyes at me and Maggie both as she walks away.

"Good morning, Mr. A," I say as he follows behind his school-appointed mentor. Maggie winks at me and, I must say, it's nice to have a homegirl backing me for a change.

"Jayd, you should come kick it with us. Mickey's leaving next week and you don't need Nellie's stuck-up ass anyway. Besides, my braids are coming loose. You can touch them up at lunch, chica." Maggie's right. Just because my girls are tripping doesn't mean I have to as well. I have plenty of prospective homies, including Maggie and her crew. So I have to keep it moving and hang with those who want to chill, and leave the rest of the folks behind.

"Okay, I'll hook you up at lunch and this one's on me."

"You hook me up right, *mami*, and I'll have a whole new clientele for you." Now that's what I like to hear. I need to be all about my money and forget about the rest of the drama.

Mickey seemed to avoid me, or maybe she just didn't want to be bothered. Either way, she and Nigel were conveniently missing in action for the day, and Jeremy didn't bother showing up to school either. So, kicking it with Maggie was a good distraction and it introduced me to a whole new population of clients, just like she said it would. Having my own car and getting off early today allowed me to get to the shop extra early this afternoon and get some much needed work done. Now that I've made sure all the clients' hair boxes are in order and my own supplies replenished, I can question Mama about what really happened on New Year's Eve.

"Mama, we never talked about New Year's Eve," I say, easing into my inquisition. If Mama didn't tell me about Misty's visit by now, she's apparently in no rush. "Anything interesting happen?"

Mama looks up from her *Ebony* magazine and at my reflection in Netta's mirror. It's been a long time since I've worked on Mama's hair and she looks like she's enjoying the treatment. Netta walks over from the sink where she's getting Mama's shampoo and conditioners ready and joins us at her station.

"Make your parts a little thinner, Jayd. We want to get her hot oil into as many nooks and crannies as possible." Mama smiles and without answering, continues to read the article on Barack Obama. Mama loves her some Barack, and so does every other female I know, with the exception of Mrs. Peterson. But she doesn't like anyone, especially not an educated black Democrat like him. Netta reaches into one of the drawers at her station and hands me a thin-handled comb with a golden point at the end for making precise parts. I need one of these in my collection.

"I see you like that comb," Mama says without looking up. At least she's talking to me.

"Yeah, she's a beauty," I say, talking about our tools like Rah talks about cars. The right comb can make or break any hairstyle, braids included. This may just be the missing link to a more perfect braid pattern. "Netta, where'd you get this comb from?" I ask Netta, who's now in the back of the shop.

"Ask your grandmother. It's hers." Mama again looks at me through the mirror and smiles. "Jayd, after you put Lynn Mae under the dryer, I need you to come back here and fill these vials with essential oils, please." Work, work, always work. I miss the days I would accompany Mama on her faithful Tuesday visits to Netta's Never Nappy Beauty Shop and just listen to the two of them talk. But now that I'm Netta's sole employee, all of that's in the past.

"Yes, ma'am," I say as I gently massage the oil into Mama's

scalp. Maybe I can relax her enough so that the truth will just slip right out of her. "So, where'd you get this fancy comb?" I ask, referring to the pretty comb now back in its drawer.

"My mother gave it to me. It was her mother's and I assume her mother's before her."

"Well, why do you keep it here instead of at home?" I continue rubbing her scalp, noticing all of the many grooves in her head. The spirit book says that no two heads are the same and I'm learning that for myself the more clients I gain.

"Because it is for my scalp only, and yours if you get your head done by anyone else. But because you do your own hair you don't need it yet."

"Really? What's so special about it?" I look at the simple, white comb with the gold handle and marvel at its strength. To have survived many tumultuous Williams women's generations it has to be made of something special.

"Well, first of all there's no other comb like it. It's made out of pure bone and gold, making it very valuable in more ways than one." Mama turns her head around and looks me in the eye, her eyes glowing. What's she looking for now?

"What kind of bone?" I ask, almost afraid of the answer. I know Mama doesn't get down like Esmeralda now, but her past is still a mystery to me.

"Why are you so inquisitive today, Jayd? What is it that you really want to ask me?" There's no use in beating around the bush with Mama. She can read my intentions like a book and with the way she's looking at me now, I feel wide open.

"Bryan mentioned something about Misty coming by Esmeralda's for New Year's." Mama turns her head back around, allowing me to continue with my work.

"Yes, she and her mother are now a part of Esmeralda's house, or spiritual lineage. And as her godchildren, they also serve as her only family, since she has no relatives that I know of." I take out the brush that matches her comb, noticing the intricately detailed pattern on the back. Where have I seen this before?

"So now she's spending holidays with her?" All I need is more Misty time to make me go completely over the edge.

"Yes, Jayd. You were blessed enough to be born into a house with an active godmother like myself, even if sometimes you don't act like it. But when you're alone, like Esmeralda, you latch on to the people who latch on to you. And in this case, Esmeralda, Misty, and her mama have become each other's family."

"But don't they know how evil Esmeralda is? And doesn't she know how evil they are?" Mama looks up at me again and frowns.

"Jayd, some people want nothing more than to be loved, and will go through all types of extremes to get it. Others simply want three things out of life: money, power, and respect, and Esmeralda happens to be one of those people. If she can find a way to use someone to get those things, she will." Mama gets up from the chair and walks over to the blow dryer, ready to relax for another fifteen minutes while the oil sets into her scalp. Then she'll get her head washed by Netta, who'll take care of the rest too.

I begin to put up the special hot oil for Mama and accidentally knock over something sitting in the corner of Netta's station. "Damn it," I say under my breath, but Mama and Netta both hear me.

"Watch it, young lady," Mama says.

"I'm sorry. I just knocked over this thing, but I don't think it broke," I say, retrieving the metal rooster with bells hanging around it. I've seen one in the spirit room, but I don't know what it's for. But whatever it is has both of them up in arms.

"Jayd, we need to do a cleansing on you before you go

home, chile. You must have a lot of negative energy around you to make this fall. If you don't act now, you'll be paralyzed before the week's out," Netta says, shutting the blinds to the shop and pulling the drapes. I can always count on Netta to be melodramatic about something simple.

"And I'm going to do a reading on you right now to see if there's anything else we need to do." Mama gets up from Netta's station and heads to the back where the shrine is located. "Netta, you can start on her head. I'll open up the cowries." I don't have time for this today. I already feel overwhelmed enough as it is, and the last thing I need is more work to do.

"Jayd, what have I told you about sassing Mama, even in your mind?"

"Mom, not now."

"It's never a good time but it's always the right time, little miss. Now, get over yourself and let them help you."

"Jayd, come on over here and let me get you settled, girl." Netta lights a cigar and breathes the smoke all over my head while chanting in Yoruba, one of the many languages of our ancestors. She then leads me to the back, where Mama is throwing the shells. She directs me to sit on the mat next to my grandmother, who is also speaking in Yoruba. Mama opens the reading and begins to speak to me.

"According to the shells, your best friend is also your worst enemy." Well I didn't need the orisha, the ancestors, to tell me that. I could've saved Mama the twenty minutes and gave her all of the info she needed by telling her about my past two days at school.

"Which one: Nellie or Misty?" Mama looks up at me and crinkles her nose like she always does when she's trying to read me. She picks up the four small pieces of coconut shell and throws them on the mat without disturbing the cowries.

"Neither." Now, I wasn't expecting that. "You're in the eye of the storm, Jayd. You'll need to make a sacrifice to clear yourself of the impending danger around you."

"Ain't that the truth," Netta adds. She looks at the shells, seeming to recognize the combination of the sixteen cowries spread across the bamboo mat. "And it came up negative, so that means you've really got to work hard to keep yourself free from this mess, and I have the perfect sacrifice for you to make." Netta practically leaps across the room to her spirit book and flips through the hefty thing until she finds what she's looking for. "Clear flow. That's what you need in your life, girl. This will keep you moving safely through a hurricane if you do it right."

"It saved me many a day," Mama says, collecting the cowries and coconut shells and placing them back in their leather pouch before returning them to Netta's shrine. I glance up at the velvet picture of the woman at the river, on the wall behind the shrine, and see the woman again looking at me through her reflection in the water. I don't think I'll ever get used to the interactive portrait.

"Here's what you need to do, Jayd," Netta says, bringing the heavy book to me. "You will need to prepare the following herbs and bathe with them tonight. When you're done, take a strainer, remove the stopper in the tub and collect as many of the herbs as you can while the water goes down the drain."

"The ones that you catch must be contained in a mason jar and disposed of in a river, stream, lake, or whatever natural body of fresh water you can find the next day, along with a petition written to Oshune," Mama adds.

"Will the ocean do?" I ask, thinking I can take care of it on my way to school in the morning.

"I said fresh water, Jayd. Mama Oshune is the one you are petitioning and she's over every other body of water. The ocean belongs to the orishas Yemoja and Olokun, but those are lessons for another day. Now, copy your cleansing ritual down and me and Netta will get back to my hair."

"But wait," I say as they leave the room. "Where am I going to find fresh water near Compton?"

"I don't know, but you have to trust your instincts. Oh, and wear white for the next three days, too. Now get to work. You have to clean the shop before we leave." Mama has no mercy on me.

After I finished my bath last night, I followed all of the in-structions and now I'm looking up fresh bodies of water to toss my offering in. I had to wrap the jar up tight in a shirt to make sure it doesn't break throughout the course of the day. Luckily, my pink jacket makes my all-white clothing look somewhat normal, but not enough for some nosy folks. I'm going to stay out of the limelight until Friday when I can re-turn to wearing other colors. Before I can get too into my re-search my phone rings. The librarian was already sweating me hard because of my bright attire; now I know she's going to freak out because of my cell.

"Hello," I whisper into the phone.

"What up, girl? Where you been hiding?" Rah asks as I try to talk to him quietly.

"Oh, nowhere. Just getting back into the swing of things. I'm looking up something in the library. Can I call you back in a few?"

"Fo sho. But make sure you call me back. I've got to talk to you about court next week."

"Okay, I will." Right as the librarian makes her way over to me, Jeremy walks in and catches my eye. Damn, he's a breath of fresh air even if I still need to holla at him about his report. But it'll have to wait until after I'm done with my mission at hand.

"You know there are no cell phones allowed in here, Miss Jackson," the old lady says, her voice trembling, like she's afraid to talk to me but more afraid of not enforcing the rules. It must be a bitch working for the system.

"I know and I'm sorry. It won't happen again."

"Well, consider this your warning." Jeremy walks up behind her and makes bunny ears over her head before she turns around and frowns up at him, too.

"Hey, Mrs. Pace. What's up?"

"Mr. Weiner," she says before walking back to her desk. Are all of the teachers up here in a perpetual bad mood or what?

"Hey, Jayd. What's up with you? And why are you wearing all white again?" he asks before reaching down to pull out the chair at the empty computer station next to mine.

"Oh, it's to help me feel better," I say, not wanting to give him the full explanation just yet. And he's learned not to press any further when it comes to some of my ways.

"What's wrong with you?" Where do I begin?

"Oh, just dealing with a lot of other people's drama. But right now I need to find a fresh body of water before the day's out and I'm having no such luck."

"Well, I know of a spot. I can take you there after school if you want." Why didn't I ask him before? If anyone knows of all the hideaway spots around here, it's Jeremy.

"Yeah, I'd like that very much. But you have to promise not to make fun of what I do when I get there," I say, ready to head to third period with him.

"Sure thing, Lady J. I've got your back, you know that." And that, I do.

It's a nice day to take a drive up the 405 freeway. I wasn't sure if my car would make it to our destination, so I allow Jeremy to take me to his fresh-water spot, which ends up being in Long Beach. Now that I can drive I need to get out and explore more. I had no idea there were beautiful lakes like this one not too far from my hood.

"Wow, how did you find this place?" I ask, exiting his car and following him to the water.

"Much exploration with much time on my hands, young one," he says, sounding like a pseudo samurai warrior. It's the most beautiful lake I've ever seen. As many times as I've been to Long Beach, I never knew about this park.

"It's perfect, Jeremy," I say, looking down at my backpack. "Well, no time like the present." I unzip my bag and take out the mason jar full of herbs.

"What's that?" Jeremy asks. His eyes focus on my hands as I unwrap the glass jar and put the shirt back in my bag, ready to symbolically rid myself of the weight I'm carrying. I shake the contents of the jar and glance at my petition, carefully folded inside. I pray that Oshune answers my prayers. I wrote down on that piece of paper everything I could think of that needs fixing and it still wasn't enough, but it'll have to do for now.

"My sacrifice," I say, looking around to make sure we don't have any spectators. The ducks on the other side of the lake don't seem interested in what we're doing at all. I guess the breadcrumbs someone left behind for them are much more captivating. I wish a similar distraction would work for Misty's nosy ass.

"Jayd, what the hell are you talking about?" Okay, he's messing up my flow and I need to be in the right state of mind for this to work.

"Jeremy, too many questions. Would you mind leaving me alone so I can get this done? I'll only be a moment." Jeremy looks at me sideways then back at the jar in my hands. Without saying another word, he leaves me at the waterside to do my thing.

I take out the chant I copied from Netta's spirit book and memorize it quickly. Apparently I need to keep my eyes on the jar until it's completely submerged in the water. Then I have to walk backwards to the car while still chanting the prayer. Here goes nothing.

"Keep it moving, keep it flowing, Oshune my mother, all-knowing. Legba, Legba, make the path clear and open the roads with my prayers for Oshune to hear." I release the jar into the calm waters, waiting for it to sink, but something's keeping it from moving. It sits still in the water, almost in the same place where I dropped it. I look around to make sure no one's watching and notice Jeremy half-asleep in his Mustang, and I'm grateful. The last thing I need is an audience. I step slightly into the water to help the jar along its way.

"Damn it," I say, pissed that my sneakers are getting wet. These are the only pair I have and they have to last me until my birthday, which is three months from now. I repeat the chant as the directions say, but cursing between refrains wasn't part of the plan if I recall correctly.

"What the hell?" This thing just won't sink. This can't be a good sign.

"Sometimes you have to be more active in your cleansings than others," my mother says. *"Pick it up and throw it as hard as you can. Get it as close to the middle as possible, Jayd. Then it'll sink for sure."*

"Thanks, Mom." I reach into the water again, this time stepping even farther to retrieve the floating jar. As I grasp the glass, I catch my reflection in the water as if looking into a moving mirror. My white bandana overshadows my facial features, which fade into the background with the rest of the image. I have the strangest feeling of déjà vu but I know it's more than that. I continue looking into the reflection and my image changes in the still water. Now I'm the woman in the picture above Netta's shrine.

"Don't get caught up in the vision, Jayd. Throw the damned jar and keep moving!" My mom's voice shakes me to my core and the vision of Maman crawling on the ground toward Mama as a baby comes into my mind and consequently into the reflection in the water. I hold on to the jar, mimicking Maman's movements precisely when she crawled away from my great-grandfather, who was trying to kill her. The vision's too powerful for me to focus on my task at hand, but I manage to throw the jar far enough and watch it finally sink away.

"Jayd, are you okay?" Jeremy asks, snapping me out of the dangerous memory and back into the present.

"Yeah, I'm fine. Just got a little wet," I say, shaking more from the vision than the chill the wind is giving me.

"Come on. I have some towels in the car." I follow Jeremy back to his car, ready to get home. That was some scary shit.

"Yes it was," my mom says, checking back in.

"Mom, what was that?"

"I don't know. That was the strangest thing I've seen you go through yet. I just hope your offering was accepted. Otherwise, you'll have more work to do to get whatever this is off you, so you can move forward. The last thing you want is to be caught up in some mess that isn't yours to begin with."

Whatever's going on, I'm going to get to the bottom of it and get me out of harm's way, come hell or high water. I may not have the money or influence that Nellie's new crew has, but I possess a lineage with the kind of power that goes beyond physical limitations. And that's the only thing I'm counting on to get me out of this twisted reality I didn't create.

~ 9 ~
The Matrix

*"So if you all keep on doing what you all are doing/
You will end up, up up in jail."*

—HORACE ANDY

It's my first day out of whites and I'm ready to take on whatever's coming my way, or so I think. Already the day's been full of drama. I'm not looking forward to the meeting with Nigel, Mickey, and Mrs. Bennett, but it's inevitable. At least it's during fourth period, Mrs. Bennett's planning time. She and the assistant principal are really tight, and he does pretty much whatever she says. Must be nice to have that kind of power when it benefits your cause.

It seems unfair that people with more influence can get away with more shit. It's also unfair that some people can get away with murder—whether literal or metaphorical—and the rest of us have to pay for it. Now I know what it means to be caught up in the matrix.

"I'm so glad you could join us, Miss Jackson," Mrs. Bennett says from her stance next to the vice principal's desk. "This shouldn't take long. We wouldn't want you to waste any more of your precious time." Why is she so snide with me all the time? You'd think she'd get tired of being a bitch and take a break for a day, but no such luck.

"Good morning, Mrs. Bennett," I reluctantly say. I nod what's up to Mickey and Nigel and sit down in the seat closest to the door and across from them. No need for me to be front and center for this conference. This is all on my friends because I'm not confessing a damn thing. And without any real proof, I should be off the hook.

"Ah, I see everyone's here," Assistant Principal Brown says, stepping into his office with a stack of papers in his hands, officially starting the meeting. I hope we get out of here before lunch. "Now, I'm sure you are all aware of the severity of the matter at hand," he says, causing Mrs. Bennett to smile big and bright. This is what gets her going, I see.

"Can I just say that I'm pregnant and have had to miss a lot of school in the past couple of months," Mickey says, rubbing her stomach with her free hand. She's been holding on tight to her man with the other one, for dear life.

"Yes, we are aware of your situation," Mr. Brown says, clearing his throat. He seems more embarrassed by Mickey's pregnancy than anyone. "Which is why going to the continuation school is the best option for you. Now, back to the matter at hand." Before Mr. Brown can continue, Nigel steps in.

"Wait a minute. Mickey's not going anywhere. We're both finishing high school right here and we'll raise our baby together." Nigel's extra sensitive now that his parents have introduced adoption as an option. And this is no way for him to find out about Mickey's new school address.

"Oh, I'm sure Mickey's already informed you of her decision. No need to be so defensive," Mrs. Bennett says, going in for the kill. I don't know how she knows, but Mrs. Bennett's hip to the fact that Mickey was keeping this important information from Nigel.

"Mickey, what the hell is she talking about?" Nigel asks, momentarily forgetting why we're really here.

"Baby, I was going to tell you later." Mickey rubs his hand gently, but Nigel can't be soothed. He abruptly pulls his hand away from hers, returning his attention to the meeting.

"Well, as I was saying. We have a serious accusation, but

without one of you confessing, we have no proof. Mickey, your parents won't return our calls or letters. Nigel, we've talked to your parents and they've assured the administration that the reins will be tightened around your neck, especially since we're counting on you for a winning football season," Mr. Brown says with a smirk on his face, but Nigel's not returning his enthusiasm.

If Nigel couldn't run fast he'd be just another black boy to Mr. Brown. But because Nigel has skills on the football field, he's got the power of the administration to back him up. His parents having money doesn't hurt, either. Influence can be bought if you're willing to pay the price. Speaking of selling out, Misty walks through the door, dropping off more paperwork on Mr. Brown's desk, not missing her opportunity to gloat a little. If it weren't for her and Nellie, we wouldn't have gotten caught in the first place.

"And Mickey, if you do decide to stay in regular school, one more absence will land you and your parents in hot water, legally. So we're all glad you made the right choice." Nigel looks at Mrs. Bennett and then at Mickey, who's near-tears she wants to cuss someone out so bad. "But forgery cannot be overlooked and neither can poisoning a student," Mrs. Bennett says, getting to why I'm present. I know she wishes she could prove that I'm the reason Laura lost her voice on the opening night of our production, but she can't. It's too bad I can't take credit for the miracle because I'm quite proud of my work.

"And Jayd, well there's not much we can do without solid proof, as you know. But because of your history and the fact that an eye-witness has come forward stating that they saw you sign Mickey's note, it can't be ignored that you were in on it. But, again we can't prove it. So, the investigation will continue until further notice."

"One step out of line young lady and you will be back on

probation, Miss Jackson," Mrs. Bennett says, taking the last word. How the hell did I get back here? I hate it when she has something to hold over my head. It's only a matter of time before she finds a way to nail me to the cross for one thing or another. I'll be damned if I'm going to let Mrs. Bennett win again. She's already humiliated me once this year and Ms. Toni is still boiling from that encounter. Now she has me in her claws again over some shit that Mickey did. This isn't right. I feel like I'm in a warped reality and I have no control over how it's turning out.

"Okay, I think we're done here. Nigel, now don't let this upset you, son. We've got an away game tonight and we're winners, right?" Mr. Brown says, standing up to give Nigel a high five, which he's left hanging on. Mr. Brown sits back down.

"May I be excused now?" Nigel asks. He looks like he wants to punch a hole in the wall.

"Yes, son, of course. You're off the hook." Nigel gets up from his seat and storms out of the office, leaving the door wide open behind him. Mickey looks at me and I shrug my shoulders. I don't know what she expected. I told her hiding this from him wouldn't go over well, just like all of her other lies. She's gotten too big for her britches, as my grandfather would say, and she's being humbled now. It's about time, even if I think Mrs. Bennett's being a bit harsh, as usual.

"And Mickey, don't forget to clean out your locker by the end of next week." Mrs. Bennett feels so powerful when she gets her way, and today she looks like she's on top of the world.

"Girls, you're free to go," Mr. Brown says. Mickey and I gladly leave the office, ready to eat lunch and just get the hell out of here. It's Friday, and I'm glad I get the weekend to recuperate from this week, today being the most eventful of them all. I'm still not sure which friend Mama was talking about becoming my worst enemy, but I'm sure that'll reveal itself in time. Right now I'm feeling like Mickey and Nellie have both done a good job of getting me into plenty of trouble, and we still have another semester to go. I don't know if I can take any more drama from my friends this year.

"Jayd, what am I going to do about Nigel?" Mickey asks, not even clear of the main office yet. She could give a damn less about her educational future or anyone else's. All that matters is her relationship with Nigel, and I've had it with this girl and her selfish behavior. We have two minutes before the bell for lunch rings and it's more than enough time for me to tell her what I think.

"What you're going to do is let this blow over. He's got a lot to process," I say, stopping short of telling her about the adoption suggestion he's also dealing with. "This is about more than just you, Mickey."

"But I can't let him think I wasn't going to tell him. I have to convince him I was right about this one," Mickey says, pulling out her BlackBerry, ready to harass Nigel into submission if necessary.

"Whatever, Mickey. I'm officially out of it," I say, walking to my locker to switch out my books for the weekend. Rah's meeting me here after school and following me to my mom's house after we handle our business. I took the afternoon off from Netta's to go to the Department of Motor Vehicles to register my hoopty, and we'll probably hang out afterwards. Kamal's spending this weekend with their grandparents, so we'll have the entire weekend to ourselves, Rahima included.

"Out of it? You can't be out of it. We're all friends and I need you now more than ever to convince Nigel not to be too mad at me."

"Mickey, are you listening to yourself? You just put Nigel in a very vulnerable position with the school, not to mention I'm on thin ice because of your shit. If we really are friends, now's the time for you to back off and let your friends cool off. Enough, Mickey," I say, slamming my locker door shut as the bell rings loudly through the empty hall. Nigel emerges from the boy's restroom and Mickey runs to him. His face is stoic and I know this isn't going to be good.

"I'll leave you two alone," I say, passing them up to go outside. Today feels like a turkey-burger-and-fries kind of day for me and I want to be the first in line. I'm hungry and not in the mood for long lines.

Fifteen minutes later we're sitting outside on our lunch break, and Mickey and Nigel have been going at it since I left them behind in the main hall. They both have valid points, but neither one is listening to the other. With them both confessing—Nigel about his parents pushing for adoption, and Mickey about hiding the fact that she's leaving the main campus next week—the heat between them is hotter than I've ever witnessed, and not in a good way.

"Mickey, how could you not tell me that they want you to leave school because you're pregnant with my baby? What type of shit is that?" The two of them are really drawing a crowd this afternoon and the spectators are loving the show, Misty and haters included. I'm surprised Misty's not busy posting up more flyers for the Valentine's Day dance next month, since I found out that she's volunteering in ASB after all.

"Baby, I didn't want you to be upset and off your game. Besides, you didn't tell me that your mama and daddy want us to give our baby away. What type of shit is that?" Mickey says, antagonizing my boy right back. Damn, this isn't good, and Chance is off who knows where with Nellie, and Jeremy isn't anywhere to be found, either.

I have no choice but to let them go at it, especially since—technically—I helped keep both their secrets. And this week I've been playing incognegro, trying to help them out of this mess and keep me from getting hurt in the midst of it. I don't know how good a job I'm doing but from the looks of it, someone's going home with some bruises and it isn't going to be me. That was the point of my recent cleansing and I'm glad to see it's working.

"Upset? Off my game? Well, lying to me doesn't help in either situation, Mickey. When were you planning on telling me? When I didn't see you at lunch one day?" Mickey looks like she wants to cry but sucks it up to save face. If it were just the two of them she'd be bawling her eyes out by now.

"Nigel, I was just trying to help. Please don't be mad at me." Mickey holds on to her man for dear life, but he's too vexed to be held right now.

"I have to get some air," Nigel says. He gets up to leave, then, doubles back for one final word. "It's my baby too, Mickey, which means I have a say in how we live, you feel me?" I've never seen Nigel so hurt before. Mickey doesn't know him like I do and to get him this hot takes a lot. Mickey's gone too far this time.

"Jayd, what am I going to do?" Mickey asks when Nigel's gone, looking to me for the answer I don't have. Just then, Chance and Nellie walk into the yard, hand in hand. Mickey follows my eyes across the grass and catches Nellie's eye, and Nellie offers a sinister smile in return. What Nellie doesn't know is that Mrs. Bennett pissed Mickey off at this morning's conference and now Mickey has nothing to lose by kicking her ass. "I'll be right back." Mickey charges across the yard toward her former best friend, ready to mow the lawn with her face.

"Mickey, don't do it!" I run after my girl but it's no use. I know she's going in for the kill. After this morning's meeting and her argument with Nigel, my girl's feeling completely powerless and needs to take it out on someone. And who better than the person she blames for it all? I wish I could end this day and start it all over again. But this isn't a movie and we have to play the scene out, however it unfolds.

"Nellie, I can't believe you would sell me out like that," Mickey says, close to reaching her destination. Misty looks on, loving the drama and the fact that my crew is falling apart. How did this happen? I feel like I'm in a twisted reality and Misty's the architect. Choosing the path of a coward, Nellie turns around and Mickey stops in her tracks, winded from the long trek. I guess that belly weight's starting to slow her down. I hope it stops her from ruining all of our lives, sooner rather than later.

After my eventful day, the last thing I want to do is go to the DMV, but business is business and I have to handle mine no matter what. Luckily I made an appointment so at least I won't have to wait in line. I filled out all of the paperwork online and printed it out to give to them. Hopefully, this will be over quickly.

Rah pulls up to the front of the school, bumping Eazy E loudly from his speakers.

"Hey, baby," he says, getting out of his seat to help me with my bags. Kamal must already be at his grandparents' house.

"Hey, you. How was your day?"

"Better than yours, or so I heard." I know Nigel already filled him in on the day's events.

"Yeah, I bet it was. Where's Rahima?" I know he's supposed to have her this weekend and I can't wait to see her.

"Sandy's dropping her off later."

"Oh." The last thing I want is to run into her.

"You can leave your car here and we'll pick it up on the way back. Your appointment's at four, in Torrance, right?"

"Yeah, that's right. I hope it doesn't take too long. It's been a long day and I'm ready to chill." I throw my backpack in his backseat and get in, glad to let him drive.

"Sounds like someone needs to take a hit," Rah says. He knows I don't smoke so he must be high himself.

"A hit of what? I know you're not talking about passing me the blunt."

"Why not, girl? You can't stay a virgin forever, you know."

"Uhm, I plan on staying a virgin for a very, very long time and in more ways than one." Rah smiles at me, laughs a little, and then turns the music up. I guess he has no comment. Rah knows better than anyone not to push that subject with me.

After handling my car business and returning to school so I could pick up my hoopty, Rah asked me to spend the evening with him and wait for Sandy to bring Rahima for the weekend. We order a pizza and settle into the melodic groove of his latest studio creation. No matter what's going on around him, Rah never gets too far out of his flow.

"That's nice," I say, biting into my Hawaiian barbeque slice while he cues up *The Last Dragon* on the DVD player. This is one of the few movies I never get tired of watching. Rah's outdone himself today. First he surprised me with flowers when I finished filing my car registration, then he filled my tank with gas and gave me money for my cell bill this month. If he keeps it up I'm going to end up asking him to get back with me, instead of the other way around. He's improved a lot lately and I'm taking notice.

"I wanted to talk to you about court next week. Are you still going to be able to come?"

"Of course I'll be there. Anything you need," I say, taking a sip of my cream soda before taking another bite of my slice.

"Well, I'm glad to hear that because my lawyer says I'd

have a better chance if I present myself as a responsible young man. But since I'm a minor and I can't get married yet, a steady girlfriend is the next best thing. So, what do you say? Will you be that girl for me?"

"Why can't you just tell him the truth, that we've been friends since junior high and I'm not going anywhere again?" I can see Rah has thought about this and I'm not going to be able to convince him otherwise.

"Jayd, it has to be steady, so I need you to say that we've been together since junior high and that Sandy was just a mistake, but you forgave me."

"Sandy was a mistake and I did forgive you, but I'm not lying to a judge about anything."

"But Jayd, you have to. Otherwise my case against Sandy will be weak."

"So that's what this day was all about? You just want me to be your surrogate wifey? Oh hell no," I say, getting up from our impromptu picnic and leaving him alone.

"Jayd, come on. What's the big deal? Trish would do it in a heartbeat."

"Well then go ask her," I say, pissed that he even brought her up.

"That wouldn't be such a good idea. Besides, you're a much better candidate."

"Candidate? I wasn't aware I was in a race." I get up, collect my shit and grab my keys from the coffee table. It's times like this I'm glad I can leave when I'm ready. "I'm sick of you using me, Rah. When will you grow the hell up?"

"Jayd, wait. Where are you going? Rahima will be here in a minute."

"I'm going home where I know where I stand, no other candidates necessary. And you can tell the judge you're single, because I'm definitely out of the picture."

"Are you calling it that?" Rah asks, watching my tears fall.

Do I really want to call it—whatever this is that we have—
quits right now? I don't feel like I do, but my head is telling
me something different. I can't let his drama keep affecting
my life.

"I don't know. Is that what you want?" I ask, not sure if I
want to write him off completely.

"Hell, no. Why would I want to burn a bridge that I might
want to walk on—or across—one day?" Rah is such the
ghetto philosopher and I love him for it. But he's got to
come with more than that to convince me otherwise.

"Rah, just leave me alone, please."

"No." Damn, it's like that? "I'm going to always be here,
whether you like it or not." I look at him and can feel his regret, but I'm still too hurt to hear him right now. First Mickey,
now Rah. What's wrong with my friends? As usual, Mama was
on point with her reading.

On my way home, I'm so pissed I can't see straight. Normally I'd call one of my girls but that's not an option tonight.
But Mama can help, and is always available for her favorite
granddaughter.

"Mama, I'm done dealing with Rah. Do you know he's
been courting me like he wants to really make our relationship work, only to find out he's been using me to make his
custody case against Sandy stronger?" I cry into my cell.

"Well, Jayd, I know he only has the best of intentions,
even if he went about it the wrong way."

"Are you defending him?"

"No, I'm defending y'all. You two have been real friends
for a long time, Jayd. Just like you, Rah's still growing up and
trying to figure his way through life, and how to resolve this
situation he's created with Sandy. I'm not saying his behavior's excusable, but I will say that he's done more right than
wrong, and you need to see it from his perspective. He's al-

ready lost his father to prison and his mama to the strip clubs. Now he's in jeopardy of losing his daughter, again. Rah's scared, Jayd, and he needs his best friend there to help him."

"Mama, it's not that simple," I say, parking in front of my mom's apartment building and turning my loud car off.

"Isn't it? When you do stupid stuff I forgive you and so does everyone else who truly loves you. All you talk about is whether or not he loves you. What about you loving him?"

"I do love him and I show him every day I'm talking to him. After he slept with Sandy behind my back and got her pregnant, I never thought I'd get over that. But I did, and we're friends again." I walk up the stairs to my mom's apartment and open the door, ready to chill for the rest of the evening. I have to be up early to get to Netta's.

"Yes, but you haven't forgiven him. And until you do that, you can never truly help him. It's like the conscious part of you knows what it wants to do but the emotional side is winning. To get through the unknown you have to let go of your emotions and trust in your path. You're in Rah's life for a reason, and vice versa. Focus on the end result, not on how y'all got to this point."

"Whenever I think we're getting closer something happens that challenges us. Why does it always have to hurt?"

"When you feel bad it's because it's getting good, which makes it even worse. It's karma in the making, Jayd, so be careful with your next move."

Mama's right. I need to consider my next step. And I'm going to stay to myself all weekend until I figure it out.

~ 10 ~
I Get Around

*"It's a lot of real G's doing time/
Cause a groupie bit the truth and told a lie."*

—TUPAC

I spent the entire weekend hustling, studying, and stacking my paper up. I even found a branch of my new bank not far from my mom's house and made another deposit. It's the first day of the last week of this semester and it can't end soon enough for me. I'm looking forward to the change.

My car made it to school this morning, but it wasn't going to make it home this afternoon. Luckily Mickey offered her brother's tools for Rah and Nigel to use to try to fix my problem, so we drove to her house. This gives me and Mickey time to catch up on our weekends, while Rah and Nigel work on my ride.

"That fool really has his nerve," Mickey says, chewing on her Chick-O-Stick like she didn't just finish three of them back to back. I finally have a chance to vent to her about Rah soliciting me as his instant girlfriend. "But you know you should do it, right?"

"That's not the point. He's been playing me like Boo Boo the fool and I've been falling for it, when all he wanted was for me to fill a vacancy. What the hell?"

"Well, he could've asked Trish to do it."

"Trish's brother is his supplier. He's already in enough debt with them and it's not a good look."

"So he wasn't trying to pimp you, really. You seem like his only option."

"I never looked at it like that." If I didn't know better, I'd say Mickey's becoming more insightful with this pregnancy. I hope it doesn't disappear once the baby's born.

"You know who you and Rah remind me of? Kim and Reggie," Mickey says, eating my entire pack of Tic Tacs at once. This girl will eat just about anything these days.

"Who the hell are Kim and Reggie?" I watch the boys working on my car and miss my uncles and Daddy doing the same back in the day. When I was younger they were always outside working on someone's car around the neighborhood. That's all said and done now. Drugs can do that to a family.

"Kim Kardashian and Reggie Bush," Mickey says, like it was the natural assumption to make.

"Whatever, Mickey. You know I never watch that show." I get my dose of reality with *Life in the Fab Lane* and *Run's House* but that's where the reality boat ends for me.

"I'm serious. They're always around each other and the family hates on her because of it. They're just haters, you feel me? And your booty's getting big like hers, and you know Rah's loving that," Mickey says, watching both of our dudes take off their T-shirts and wipe the sweat from their foreheads. Rah's gray wife beater's hugging up against his chest, making the heat in my body rise to my cheeks. I may still be mad at him, but damn, he's fine. Nigel's white tank looks pretty good up against his chocolate skin too, but his powers only work on Mickey and Nellie.

"I know you're not talking about anyone's behind, Missy Elliot," I say, pushing Mickey's shoulder with mine. It's a nice evening to sit outside. The families on her block are watering their lawns and walking their mutts, much like they're doing on my block right now. It feels strange not being at home at this time of evening. Having a car does change things.

"Yeah, but it's different with me. I'm expecting. My ass is bound to spread a little. But my boo keeps me draped in clothes and will for the entire pregnancy. I can't wait until we're married and we buy our first house. My closet's going to be the size of another room." This girl is still dreaming, I see. She and Nigel spent the weekend making up after their bitter fight last Friday.

"If Nigel's parents have anything to say about it, you and Nigel are going to end up without a family, Juno," I say.

"What are you saying? That me and Nigel are going to give away our baby? That'll never happen. Ever," she says adamantly. Being married with children is Mickey's biggest want in the whole world and I know she's not giving in to that frame of mind.

"Why are y'all looking so serious over there?" Rah asks, coming up for air from underneath the hood of my ride.

"Because it's serious shit, man. I need some food. How much longer are y'all going to be under there?" Mickey asks.

"As long as it takes," Rah says, smiling at me. It was very sweet of him to come to Compton after school and help out Nigel with my car, especially since we're technically not talking. Mickey's brothers are good, but they take forever to get the simplest thing done. They have no respect for time, which is why they're always doing time, in my opinion.

"You got some chocolate or something in that bag of yours?" Mickey asks, snatching my purse and rummaging through it. Mostly I have receipts, scrunchies and loose change floating through my bag, which she's finding out now.

"Why, you want some chocolate?"

"Yes, I do," she says, continuing her search.

"Well, I don't have any." She looks up at me, disappointed and frustrated.

"Why didn't you just say that instead of allowing me to dig through all of this shit?"

"Because you didn't ask until you were already violating my stuff." I snatch my multicolored hobo back and look at Mickey like she's lost her damn mind.

"Come on, baby. I'll take you to get something to eat. Rah's got this part anyway," Nigel says, tossing his towel on the ground next to one of the toolboxes. He grabs his shirt off the top of my car and heads over to where we're sitting to help Mickey up. She's milking this pregnancy for all it's worth and I don't blame her because Nigel's loving it, too.

"Yeah, we're going to have to come back another day and finish, Jayd. We need some extra parts and the sun's setting, taking our light with it." Mickey's garage isn't a full-service auto shop so there's no outside light to help them see what they're doing.

"Damn, that means I'm going to have to leave my car here." And that also puts me back on the bus until my ride is ready. Ain't this some bull?

"Come on, babe, it could be worse," Rah says, rising from the ground and wiping his face with a towel before tossing it down next to Nigel's. "At least you have a car to leave somewhere."

"Yeah, but the point is that because I have a car I should be able to get around good. Now I'm pretty much back where I started," I say, rising from my seat on the top porch step, ready to head in for the night. I have mad homework to get through and I have to work at Netta's tomorrow, which means I need to be prepared should I have a quiz.

"Not really. You have a license to drive any car, not just your own. Look at the big picture," Rah says, trying to cheer me up, but I'm still hurt that he tried to use me. I haven't decided if I'm going to stand up with him at his hearing or not, but if I do it won't be because of my love for him but rather because of my love for Rahima. "Come on. Let's get out of here before the devil shows up," he says, referring to Mickey's man. I'm surprised Mickey left school with Nigel. They're getting really bold to be sneaking around.

I'm glad today was a short day but I hate that I'm back on the bus. I need to call my daddy before I get all the way to Netta's shop. The last thing I want is to hear their teeth sucking when they find out I'm talking to my daddy about the trifling car he bought me. I've spent most of my money from doing hair and working at Netta's on my car, and it's going to cost even more to get the parts for Rah and Nigel to finish it. Mickey's brother says he knows someone who can get them for half price, but I don't want to go that route. Who knows what stolen car he gets his parts from.

After exiting the bus, I reach into my purse and pull out my slender cell to see another text from Rah, singing his apologies. I'm going to call him Usher from now on, as much as he's trying to confess his wrongdoings to me and our friends. Nigel and Mickey have even gotten involved in the text fest and I'm tired of it. None of them pay my bills and free text messages aren't included in my calling plan.

Rather than return Rah's umpteenth text today, I scroll down to my dad's number and press send. After letting it ring several times, he finally picks up. He's dodged my last two calls and I didn't leave a message because I can tell when he's avoiding me. I've already told him my car is trippin' so he knows what's up.

"Hey, girl," he says, sounding like he was asleep. I wouldn't be surprised if he was. He's the manager at the Infiniti car lot he works at, so he basically makes his own hours, leaving his afternoons free to lounge if he so chooses.

"Hey, Daddy. What's up with you?" I ask, trying to make small talk before I go in for the kill.

"Nothing much. Why don't you leave messages when you call so I can know what the call was about?"

"I'm your daughter. Just the fact that I called should be enough for you to call back, no?"

"No, it isn't. So I assume this is about *your* car," he says, stressing the fact that it's my car now, outright. I made the mistake of telling him that Rah and I changed the registration over from his name to my name and I ordered my personalized plates. By the time they get here I don't know if I'll have a car to put them on, but I'll still have them as proof that I had my own wheels. I'm only a block away from Netta's shop and I need to wrap this conversation up before I get to work.

"Yes, it is. The last time we talked you said you'd help me get it fixed. I've already spent three hundred dollars on the thing and I need your share." After a few moments of silence, he takes a deep breath before responding.

"Jayd, it's enough that I bought the thing and paid for your first month of insurance, not to mention the driving lessons and the full tank of gas I sent you back to your Mama's house with. Do you know how much gas costs these days?" The tears in my eyes begin to swell. I can tell where this conversation's going.

"Daddy, it's never worked. How are you going to give me a broken gift that I have to get fixed?"

"Having a car is a responsibility, Jayd. And if you're not ready for that responsibility you can take the bus like you've been doing. Besides, where do you really need to go? Your job is walking distance from your grandmother's house and your little boyfriends can take you everywhere else you need to go." Who does he think he's talking to, Nellie?

"Daddy, you can't be serious. You'd rather me get rides from dudes than provide me with safe transportation?"

"You're just like your mother, you know that? Always twisting up my words and taking things out of context. Ungrateful kids these days, boy I tell you," he says to no one in particular. "Ask your grandmother for the money. Everyone knows she's sitting on a fortune." How does he know about Mama's money? I stop short of the shop to finish my conversation and collect myself. I don't want Mama to see me crying over this mess. She warned me, as well as my mom and Netta, but I didn't listen. And now I'm paying the price and stuck with the aftermath.

"Mama's not sitting on anything and besides, it's not her responsibility to provide me with transportation. I have parents."

"I give your mother enough money monthly for your bus pass. The car and the lessons were extra, Jayd, and until you get that, I'm done with the matter. Enjoy the rest of your day," he says before leaving me hanging. Damn, he's cold.

"What's up, baby girl? Can a brotha holla?" Mickey's man says through his cracked-open, tinted window. I didn't even hear the Monte Carlo pull up next to me. My dad's got me all off. "I thought Mickey's brothers were fixing your car. Need a ride?"

"Oh hell, no. I got it," I say, resuming my walk to Netta's shop. I'm in the side parking lot connecting Netta's Never Nappy Beauty Salon to the gas station, and Mickey's man is right beside me.

"You ain't got to say it like that," he says, pulling his car in front of me and blocking my strut. What does he want now?

"Can I help you with something?" I ask, putting my hands on my hips, ready to tell his ass off. I just need to give him one good cuss-out and maybe he'll leave me alone.

"Yes, you can. I told you I wanted your psychic ass to tell me if my baby's having my baby or some other nigga's. If so, you know I have to handle that, and I just want to be sure I pop the right fool for messing with what's mine." He licks his lips and gives me a look that sends shivers down my spine. The other two cars in the gas station ignore the scene because it's nothing unusual. I want to scream murder even though it hasn't happened yet. Just the mention of him shooting a gun brings my dream of him shooting at Nigel back to my mind, front and center.

"I'm not psychic. And if I were I wouldn't tell you shit," I say. I try to walk around the car but he reaches through his now fully opened window, grabbing the string on my backpack and pulling me to him. Oh no, this fool didn't. I slap his arms and he enjoys playing with me.

"Temper, temper," he says, pulling me around to face him. "But that's okay. I like my girls with a little spice in them." He smiles at me as I struggle to get free from his grip. He grabs my left arm with his free arm, pulling me down to his level, and holds me close to the door like he's going to kiss me. It's times like these I wish I were taller so I could knee him in the nose and run for it.

"Let me go, punk. My family's right through that door and if I scream you're going back to jail for a long ass time."

"You think I'm scared of you, little girl? I've been around this block a long time and ain't nobody ever kept me from what I want until your little high-and-mighty ass came around introducing Mickey to other men. I say you owe me. What you think?" His beer-ridden breath is hot against my neck as he pulls me in closer. How did I get in this weak position?

"I'm only going to ask you one more time," I say, gearing my nails up to scratch the shit out of him until he lets me go. I don't want to antagonize him any more than he already is, but I'll be damned if he's going to get the best of me, especially in broad daylight.

"You tell your boy Nigel that his days are numbered, you hear me? And we'll continue our conversation about how you can make all of this up to me another time, preferably in private while you're braiding my hair, as well as other activities I've got planned for us." He pushes me away from his car and speeds off. Mickey's messing around has landed us all in hot water and her man's the fire up under all our asses. She needs to come correct with him and stop sneaking around before we all end up dead.

"Jayd, what took you so long, girl? And where's your car?" Netta asks, lining up all of Mama's hair tools at her station. Mama must be in the back. I'm glad too, because I can't look her in the eye right now. She'll see everything written all over my face. I need a moment to straighten myself out before facing her.

"It's at Mickey's house. Rah and Nigel are going to finish it as soon as I can get the money for the parts. Until then, I'm back to busing it. I'm surprised Mama didn't tell you," I say, closing the front door and walking to the locker with my name on it. I can hear Mama in the back washing her hands.

"No, she hadn't gotten around to it yet. She was running late this afternoon. Something about the bank," Netta says. Mama has endless errands, among other things that she does all day long, which are unknown to me.

"There's my girl," Mama says, walking out of the bathroom and giving me a hug. She feels so warm and smells so sweet, her embrace makes me instantly feel better. What would I do without my grandmother's love? I don't know, and I never want to find out. "How was your day, baby?"

"It was okay. Just glad to be here," I say, not wanting to let her go. Mama lets me hug her a little longer before pulling away and forcing my chin up to look at her before letting go.

"So, how's the car faring?" She takes her customary seat in front of Netta's station, ready to get her hair done. Her crown's getting so long she's now wearing it in a long bob that grazes her shoulders. Her natural salt-n-pepper color perfectly compliments her latest style, and makes Mama look ten years younger, and she already looks younger than her fifty-plus years.

"It's not. I've spent most of my money on the thing and it still needs a lot more work."

"Did you ask your daddy to help?" Netta asks. Mama can tell from my eyes that I've already been down that road. "Of course you did," Netta says, now in the loop.

"Oh, Jayd, I'm sorry you've been disappointed again, baby," Mama says. "If I could kick your daddy's ass again without going to jail, I would," Mama says, making me laugh.

"Lynn Mae, you know you can get to that man if you really wanted to and no one would be the wiser," Netta says, clamping the cold flat iron before setting it down next to the oven. I still have to do my mini cleansing before officially beginning my work. After my encounter with Mickey's man, I really need to get my energy purified.

"My dad's tripping," I say, wiping the tears from my eyes with the back of my jacket. I take it off and hang it up next to my backpack, then retrieve my personalized apron and put it over my head, ready for work. These dudes have slowed me down enough today.

"Tell me something I don't know," Mama says, looking at me while Netta parts her scalp. I know she knows something else is up with me, but I'm not telling her about my encounter in the parking lot right now. That can wait for another day when I'm not so emotional.

"Well, I still haven't decided if I'm going to pretend to be Rah's baby-mama-in-waiting for the judge tomorrow," I say, dropping yet another bombshell. It's been an eventful week and it's only Tuesday. I haven't decided what I'm going to do about that situation and I know I can't leave my boy hanging much longer.

"Wow, little queen. You've got a lot on your plate. And don't you have your school finals this week, too?" At least Netta remembers my school schedule. Mama wouldn't know what semester it was if I didn't remind her.

"Well, luckily in my AP classes we have term papers due. So that only leaves my math and dance class where I have finals tomorrow, and I have an open-book exam on Friday in my Spanish class. I should be okay as far as my grades are concerned." I don't know what I got in government class, but it can't be less than a B, and I know I got an A in English. And I never worry about my steady A in drama class. Our final was the Fall Festival. We'll chill until the next play, which isn't for a couple of months. "It's Mickey and her drama I'm still worried about."

"That boyfriend of hers thinks he owns her," Netta says. "And that's because she allowed him too much power over her."

"I have no sympathy for that fast-ass girl. She knew what she was doing when she did it and now she has to pay the consequences. I just hope no one else gets dragged into her mess."

"Mama, that's a bit harsh," I say, cleaning all of the combs in the sink.

"Well, it's the truth. She gives young mothers everywhere a bad name. Instead of focusing on how she and her baby are going to make it, she's still playing games with these boys. When is she going to get serious?"

"I agree with you one hundred percent, Lynn Mae. Babies don't wait for their parents to get a clue. They have a way of being born whether or not folks are ready for them." Rahima's a perfect example of that fact of life.

"All Mickey thinks about these days is locking Nigel down, but his parents are never going to let that happen."

"I know they're not and I think that's the best way to handle the situation," Mama says.

"Why? If they want to be married why shouldn't they have the right to be?" I ask, but I already know the answer.

"Because she doesn't know whose baby she's carrying,

that's why." Netta says, taking the words right out of Mama's mouth and my mind. "That's old-school pimping, baby girl, and that game's not so easy to play anymore. They have paternity tests to clear all of that up now."

"And until they do, Nigel needs to deal with Mickey very delicately. That little fool-ass boyfriend of hers is no joke. I still blame him for getting Pam strung out." Mama's forehead crinkles and I know she's worried about Pam, our neighborhood crackhead. We haven't seen her in a couple of weeks and she's usually around to collect one of Mama's hot plates at least once a week. "Never put yourself in a position where someone can control you because they feel you owe them something. That's what your mom did with your daddy and you see where that's gotten us all."

Yeah, in a perpetual state of drama, and I for one intend to break this cycle. There are some lessons that come hard and some that I get the first time around. Dealing with controlling dudes is a big no-no in my book, and I'm not keeping this lesson for the next lifetime. I just hope Mickey gets it this time around, too. She needs to let go of the past for the sake of her baby and everyone around her. Otherwise, we're bound to keep repeating this bull over and over again.

~ 11 ~
Mine to Keep

"... it ain't what you cop / It's about what you keep."

—LAURYN HILL

After talking to Mama and Netta yesterday, I decided to be a compassionate friend and accompany Rah to his hearing, even if I don't want to go. I'm not sure I'll ever be able to completely trust Rah like I did when we first met years ago. When he's not honest with me I question his true intentions and that's not good for any relationship. But, he's a friend I love and intend on keeping around, so we're just going to have to find a way to work this out.

I'm just glad I get to leave school after lunch to attend the hearing. Today's a good day to be gone anyhow, with half the school conveniently absent as the semester winds down, Jeremy included. I haven't talked to him since he took me to the lake last week and I'm not looking forward to running into to him today, should he show up. I know Chance told Jeremy about me being back in hot water with Mrs. Bennett and I don't want to hear his mouth about it. I don't care if she is his favorite teacher; Jeremy's judgment concerning Mrs. Bennett is still questionable to me.

"What's up, Lady J?" Jeremy says, surprising me as he falls in step with me.

"Nothing much. Is school out already?" I ask, noticing he doesn't have any books with him.

"These last days are just technicalities. After today I won't be back until Monday. My last final's this afternoon and the rest of the week looks good for surfing."

"It's only sixty-five degrees outside and I know the water's got to be much colder than that. How is that perfect?"

" 'The sun is shining, the weather is sweet,' " he says, in the worst white-boy imitation of Bob Marley I've ever heard.

"Yeah, okay. You're not immune to the elements, you know."

"Neither are you," Jeremy says, noticing my long, black sweater dress with panty hose to match. I'm wearing socks over them with my sneakers around campus, but my matching black heels are in the car. I wanted to look as professional as possible for the hearing this afternoon, but I also need to be comfortable while I'm here. "You look nice. Going somewhere special today?"

"Not really," I say, avoiding a straight answer. I wish my plans were to chill like him but that's a day I'm not counting on happening anytime soon. "We all can't just up and leave school when we want." Jeremy looks down at me and smiles, reminding me just how attractive he is. His baseball cap can barely fit over his thick, golden-brown curls that compliment his blue eyes, making me forget what we're talking about. The bell for second period rings, snapping me back to reality, but Jeremy heads in the opposite direction of his class. "Aren't you worried about your absences?"

"It's a new semester, which means a clean slate, absences and all. I'm not worried about it."

"Must be nice," I say.

"It is. I'll catch you third period. I've got to make a quick change to my schedule," he says, disappearing into the break crowd.

I can't wait to get my car back this afternoon, although I'm not looking forward to being back over at Mickey's house, especially after running into her man last week. After the hearing, Rah and I are going to reclaim my vehicle.

Rah and I arrived at the courthouse early, just to make sure we got here on time. Part of being responsible is not being late, and Rah's proven that he's good with time already. Now it's the rest of the requirements we have to meet.

"Jayd, I really appreciate you doing this for us, baby," Rah says, nervously holding my hand under the table we're seated at, waiting for Sandy and the judge to appear. Both attorneys are present and waiting with us. "I wonder what's taking them so long?"

"I don't know. But hopefully they'll be here soon." I've never seen Rah so nervous. He's kind of cute like this.

"Excuse my tardiness, but we have a situation in the hall," the judge says, poking her head through the door.

"What kind of situation?" Sandy's attorney asks, the first to stand up. Rah's attorney stays seated and instructs us to do the same.

"Come get your client. She's refusing to come into the room. She said she wanted to speak with me alone and I obliged, but now she's become irate and I can't handle her." I knew Sandy would pull something like this. When the attorneys informed us that she and the judge were in the judge's chambers I knew it wasn't going to be a good day. I just hope it's nothing like the dream I had about her taking Rahima. I pray that the brownies we made for Rah work, and keep the good luck on our side no matter what kind of fool Sandy acts like.

"In light of the situation, I'm going to proceed in granting the request that's been filed for joint custody until we can establish grounds for giving one parent sole custody. This hearing is adjourned." Well damn, that was the quickest decision

I've ever seen, but from the way the attorneys went with it I guess it's pretty standard in these cases.

"I know it's not what you asked for, but at least it's on record now that you have rights too, and she can't just up and leave without you knowing about it anymore," Rah's attorney says. She looks down at her ringing cell and answers it, leaving us alone.

"Yeah, I guess," Rah says, sounding deflated. Sandy always has a way of making shit all about her and today was no exception. "Let's go get your ride." I hold Rah's hand as we walk out of the small room behind the main courtroom, which is where we're going to end up eventually, knowing Sandy's crazy ass. When we get outside, Sandy and her attorney are talking loudly. We try to avoid them, but there's not a chance.

"He's mine and so is his baby. You know that, right Jayd?" Sandy says to me as rudely as possible. You'd think she'd act better when the threat of losing her child is right in front of her face.

"Sandy, shut up talking to Jayd and act like you have some sense for a change," Rah says. Sandy's attorney tries to regain her focus but Sandy's on one and doesn't plan on stopping her tirade.

"I will not shut up talking to her if I don't want to. I can keep it up for a lifetime, Jayd. Remember that."

"Let's just go, Rah. Forget about her. I have," I say, loud enough for her to hear.

"Mine, Jayd. It's my life you're trying to live and I'm not going to let you have it."

"You don't have any choice in the matter because, just like you, I'm not going anywhere," I say, turning around and following Rah to the parking lot. I'm keeping my friend around, no matter how huge a mistake he made with Sandy. As long as we're together, I can handle her and anything else that comes our way.

Rah and Nigel have been working on my car for the past two hours and they say they're almost finished. I don't know how true that is, but we're having a pretty good afternoon and I don't have any homework tonight to worry about. It's not so bad hanging out, even if I am worried about Mickey's man pulling up.

"You look so cute C-walking, but you're still doing it wrong," Mickey says to her little brother Mikey who is trying his best to get the gangster dance down. "Jayd, show him how it's done."

"I haven't tried C-walking in a long time," I say, getting up and joining Mikey on the front lawn. I put my hands in the air and rise up on my tiptoes, crip-walking as best I can in my pantyhose and sneakers.

"Ah, go head, shawty. You got it," Mickey says, laughing at me. "Let me see if I can get that." I miss hanging out with Mikey. Ever since he entered junior high he's been hard to catch up with. I just hope Mickey's man doesn't get him or anyone else out in these streets. He's a good kid and I'd hate to see him go the wrong way.

"Jayd, you're just showing off now," Rah says, looking up from under the hood of my car and smiling. Rah taught me how to crip walk and Mikey looks impressed that I can get down.

"What set you from?" Mikey asks, playing around with me. But claiming hoods is no joke around here. We're in Blood territory and he knows I stay on the blue side of town. I'm sure he rarely rolls to the Nutty Block side of Compton where I live.

"Me phi me, fool," I say, imitating some of the college boys KJ used to hang out with who refused to pledge a fraternity.

It's all the same to me—fraternity, sorority or gang. They're all about giving up your solo identity to be a part of some group where someone else is the leader, and I'm not down with any of that shit and never will be.

"I got to pee. I'll be right back," Mickey says, walking into the house. I continue dancing to the southern rap blaring from Nigel's twenty-twos. None of us notice at first when Mickey's man's Monte Carlo pulls around the corner. Damn, I hate running into this fool.

"You look good doing that gangster shit, girl," he says to me through his window. Tre, my old homeboy and neighbor, is in the passenger's seat and looks as high as a kite. "Who's the nigga?"

"That's Rah," I say, looking toward my car. I hope Nigel has sense enough to stay under the other side until Mickey gets back out. Her little brother goes in the garage after nodding "what's up" to Mickey's man. If Rah pops his head back out it's liable to go down between him and Mickey's man. They've never gotten along.

"I'm not talking about him. I'm talking about the other fool over there. Is that the Nigel I've been hearing so much about?"

"Nah, that ain't Nigel. That's my homie, Brad. He's just helping Rah work on my car," I lie. Mickey comes back outside, looking from her man to Nigel's feet and then at me, trying to figure out what's really going on. Before she has a minute to plan her next move, I tip her off to our innocent game. "Mickey, Rah and Brad are almost done," I say, and she immediately catches on. Nigel's dad is right: Mickey would be good at hustling in a game of pool. But without me to help her, she'd be caught in the act for sure. Just then both Rah and Nigel emerge to see we have company.

"Hey Nigel, you want to play after you're done?" Mickey's little brother says, tossing a football in the air and blowing our cover. Nigel and Mickey both turn gray as Mickey's man goes for his glove compartment. How does he go riding around strapped when he's under house arrest? Does he value his freedom at all?

Just as my dream predicted, Mickey's man pulls out his nine and starts busting rounds Nigel's way. But unlike my dream, Nigel's not in his car and can't get away fast enough.

"Gun!" I yell and everyone hits the ground and ducks for cover. I'll never forgive Mickey for this shit.

Tre and Mickey's man open their doors and run toward Nigel and Rah, who now are back in Rah's Acura where I know Rah's got his piece too. I hate this shit. Rah jumps out and fires a few rounds in return but Mickey's man is already too close. Tre, noticing it's my homie from back in the day that Mickey's man is shooting at, looks at me, confused. He knows Nigel's a good brotha and so is he. I look at Tre and plead with my eyes for the shooting to stop. Just then, Tre jumps in front of Nigel to try to stop Mickey's man from killing him and catches the bullet instead. Rah shoots at Mickey's man again, this time catching him in the shoulder.

"My man!" Mickey screams, running toward the tragic scene. It's not clear which man she's referring to, but both of them are in pretty bad shape from what I can see. How did this happen? One minute we're kicking it and dancing and the next we're running from gunshots.

"Shit," Mickey's man yells, getting back behind the wheel of his ride. Trying to get away, he runs his car straight into the light pole and is knocked out cold.

The cops get here just in time, and thank God, because even with Tre taking the bullet, it still hit Nigel and they're both losing blood quickly. Rah's okay and hides his piece in the garage before we embrace, grateful we're okay.

* * *

Yesterday's shooting has been the talk of the city. Brandy and her sister spent the night at the hospital with their brother, and Tre didn't make it. Mickey's man will probably be locked up for a while, and that's good news for Mickey and Nigel. The word is out now that Mickey's maybe baby-daddy is Nigel, and they couldn't be happier, but his shoulder having a bullet in it isn't good news.

Tre wasn't one of my favorite people, but we did grow up together. He was always included in hide-and-go-seek, freeze tag, and playing house, which was his favorite of all our childhood games. Speaking of childhood, Misty and her mom are also here at Brandy's house to show their respects. Tre was Misty's first kiss. I forgot all about that. We were at her house playing spin the bottle and when he spun, Misty was the target. She was sprung on him for the rest of the summer and he liked her booty.

Tre used to ball with Rah and Nigel at the park back in the day, but he left the court for the streets. The hustle called him for a long time and eventually, he answered. I thought when he got out of jail this time he would turn his life around. But like the spirit book says in one story, sometimes the dark path must be lived out so that one can return to the light the next time around. Mama didn't come and I knew she wouldn't. This hits too close to home for her.

My uncles have all had their fair share of run-ins with death by way of guns. Mama's had to petition Ogun—the orisha over guns, other weapons, and war—on many occasions on behalf of her sons. And, after my dream about the drive-by and her dream about bloodshed, I know she's been visualizing this for a minute and doesn't need to participate in the reality of the moment.

Misty begins to head over toward us and I know it's not to give me a hug.

"Did you have something to do with this too, Jayd?" Misty

asks, loud enough to stop people from talking about what a good boy Tre was, even though we all know the truth. I know Misty's in shock, but she can't be serious.

"Misty, not here, not now," I say, trying to calm her down. Going off in front of me at school is one thing. But bringing that shit home ain't right. Her mother grabs her by the arm and wisely directs her to keep moving.

"Not now, but soon, Jayd." Usually her threats don't scare me, but there's something else behind that one. I'm going to have to watch out for Misty a little closer, especially since she's hanging out with Esmeralda.

After staying home yesterday and cleansing with Mama and Netta, I'm not feeling like being back at South Bay High. When someone gets shot, time seems momentarily suspended. And because Nigel is one of my oldest friends, I'm really not here with everyone else.

With it being the last day before the new semester begins, everyone was too busy cleaning out their desks and finalizing new schedules to take the day too seriously. The news spread like wildfire that Nigel was dead, paralyzed, or permanently blind, none of which is true. Nigel's bullet was successfully removed from his shoulder, but there may be permanent damage in his right arm, and that's not good news. Mickey can't even see him because his parents have barricaded him inside his room and made it clear that she's not welcome. Now Mickey's going off on me like it's all my fault and I can't take anymore.

"You got my homeboy shot, Mickey. If anyone should be pissed it's me, and believe me, I am. I'm just trying to be cool about it." Mickey stops in her tracks right in front of my locker looking shocked at my words. Whatever. I'm just telling the truth and it's about time she heard it.

"First of all, I didn't get anyone shot. Niggas are crazy,

Jayd, and that ain't my fault. Second of all, Nigel's my man. If anyone's in mourning it's me. Do you know what will happen to us if he can't play ball anymore?"

"Mickey, you've known him for what, three months?" I say, looking down at her belly. "I've known him for five years and we've been through a lot together. But never did I worry about him getting shot until he met you." Mickey looks genuinely hurt by my words and I'm glad they're finally getting through that thick skull of hers. "I'm pissed, Mickey, and I'm worried about Nigel. I could care less about how you're going to make it out of this situation because this ain't about you. This is some shit Nigel can't give back, and you can't take it back. This reality is here to stay and we have to deal with it, which means I have no time for your trifling-ass problems. Maybe it is best that you go to the continuation school. We need a break from your selfish ass." I turn around and open my locker, ready to clear it of this past semester. One down and one to go.

"So what was this fight all about?" my mom asks as we eat our In-N-Out burgers before she's out for the weekend. I fill her in on my week and on the fact that now I'm officially rolling solo as far as my girls are concerned. Rah went to visit Nigel, and I took the bus to Inglewood today.

"Mickey opened her big mouth and lies came out. She should've just told the truth and none of this would've happened."

"Nah, she should've been more careful with her creeping, if you know what I mean. Some things you just don't tell," my mom says in a cryptic voice. She's remembering something but I can't tell what it is. Sometimes I wish her powers over me worked the other way around. "Sex is a powerful thing."

"That's why I'm not giving up my cookies no time soon," I

say. "I'm not giving it up to anyone until I'm sure it's all mine to keep." My mom stops eating and looks up at me in complete disbelief.

"Yours to keep? Once you give it up, Jayd, it's gone and there's no getting it back, no matter what you may have heard," my mom says. "It's not a shirt."

"And that's my point. If I'm not sure that my cookies can stay with me no matter who I choose to give them to, I'm not giving them up, plain and simple." That's too much ashe going everywhere without my consent, as Mama would say, and I hear her loud and clear. "Wouldn't it be nice to have relationships where kissing is enough?" I say, nostalgic for the times when Rah and I would sneak behind the bleachers and kiss in junior high. We eventually got caught and promptly punished for passionate kissing, which wasn't allowed anywhere at our stark Christian school.

"Jayd, you're not still a virgin are you?" my mom asks as she rises from where we're eating on her bed and continues packing her weekend bag for another adventure with Karl. I look at my mother, shocked she's so surprised. "Girl, the way you and Rah carry on I thought you two had slept together already. Y'all really had me fooled," she says, buzzing around her room like she's in a whirlwind.

"No, Mom, I didn't give up my cookies to him or anyone else," I say, taking another bite of my burger. I won't be hungry when I get to Rah's later on.

"Well, here's something to carry, just in case you change your mind," she says, passing me a gold-wrapped condom.

"I don't need this," I protest, but my mom's already out of the room and headed toward the bathroom.

"You never know what you'll need until you're already in the moment. Trust me, girl, it's better to be safe than sorry." Well, I can't argue with her there. Look at Mickey and her mess. Had Nigel strapped his soldier up we wouldn't be on the front line of their war as we speak.

I'm ready for my date with Rah and his daughter, celebrating him winning joint custody of his little girl. But when I get off the bus and to the house, there's anything but celebrating going on outside.

"Rah, this is some bull and you know it. If I want to leave with my daughter I can be up and out anytime I damn well please." Sandy reaches for Rahima but luckily she's sleeping through the drama in her daddy's arms.

"Sandy, get off of my property now before I call the police." Too bad he's just bluffing. Rah doesn't want the cops at his house any more than Sandy does, and she knows it, which is why she keeps talking shit.

"So what y'all doing tonight? Having a little family reunion? Only problem is, the guest of honor came out of me, not you, little heffa." That's all I can take. After the shooting and dealing with the rest of Mickey's madness, I need to let it out.

"Sandy, what will it take to make you shut the hell up, for real? I mean, I'm willing to pay your ass, do your hair for free, anything to keep your mouth from moving for a day." Shocked at my bold statement, Sandy's momentarily silent. I walk over to Rah, who bends down to give me a kiss. After what happened with Nigel, we know who our true friends are and we don't have any more time to waste on those who aren't in it for real.

"Hey, baby. How you feeling?" Rah says, ever worried about me breaking down because of Tre's death and Nigel's gunshot wound. But I'm not going to break down if I can help it.

"I'm good. How are you?" I answer while he passes Rahima to me without waking her up.

"Uhm, hello," Sandy says, still here. I almost forgot she was standing there for a minute. I wish she were always that ignorable. "I still need a ride home. Are you going to take me or what?"

"Why can't you get back the same way you got here?" Rah asks, stating the obvious.

"I got here on the bus, and if you want me gone, you'll have to come out the pocket." I look back into the garage and notice Rah's grandfather's classic, silver Regal parked in there, and Rah's eyes follow. I didn't know he was finished working on it. Damn, that was fast. Too bad my car couldn't be repaired that fast. After the shooting, Rah and I dropped it off at Netta's. It only needs one more part and then I should be able to drive it again until the next time it breaks down.

"That's supposed to be a surprise. It's my way of saying thank you." Rah reaches in his pocket and hands Sandy a twenty and me the keys to his car. "You can roll the Acura until we find something else more suitable for you and I'll roll the Regal."

"Oh hell, no," Sandy says. "I know you're not going to let me, the mother of your child, ride the bus home while you give this girl, who ain't even giving you none, the keys to your car. What the . . ."

"Not in front of Rahima, Sandy. Enough's enough." Rah's had it and so have I.

"You know what, you're right. Here, take them. If it'll get you out of here for now, go on and take the Acura," I say, giving her the keys.

"Jayd, are you sure?" he asks.

"You gave it to me for now, right? Then I say yes to peace. Now, where were we?" I have a long day at Netta's ahead of me tomorrow and it's been a long week. The sooner I get Sandy out of here, the better.

"Fine. Bye," Sandy says, snatching the keys out of my hand

and walking to the red car. Rah watches her as she claims the seat, taking off and finally leaving us alone. Now we can chill for the rest of the evening.

Rahima slept through the night and woke us up bright and early for breakfast this morning. I still have some time before I have to get to work, but not much. Sandy was supposed to bring the car back this morning, but she's not here yet.

"Let me hook you up real quick before I have to go," I say, scratching his scalp.

"I didn't think you had time for your boy now that you're doing everyone else's hair."

"You know this head right here is mine to keep. You better not let anyone else touch your hair, ever." Rah pulls me down onto his lap and kisses me like I'm his woman. I guess our posing for the judge wasn't all for show.

"Well, isn't this cozy?" Sandy says, sneaking up on us. Giving her the keys was not the best idea, I see.

"What are you doing here so early? I thought you said you'd pick Rahima up this afternoon for the birthday party?" Sandy called after she left last night, saying she forgot about some kid's party she promised to take Rahima to. She's supposed to bring her back right after, but Rah didn't trust her and volunteered to take them and pick them up.

"Well, I need to take her shopping first, which reminds me. I need fifty dollars to get her some new gear."

"I just bought her clothes for Christmas. I'm not giving you any more money." And I also got her an outfit so I know the child's not in need of anything.

"Whatever. Where is she? We have to get to the mall before it gets crowded."

"She's taking her morning nap. You'll have to wait," Rah says, unmoved.

"I'm going to holla at my boy around the corner. Call me when she wakes up."

"Hey, you know that car ain't yours, right? Don't get too comfortable."

"Oh, I won't, don't worry. I don't want anyone's left-overs." She could've fooled me.

"As a matter of fact, you can walk around the corner. Leave the keys on the counter. I'll call you when she wakes up." Sandy walks out of the studio and back through the house. Finally. Now I can braid his hair real quick before I really start my day. We want to check on Nigel after I get off and I want to make something special to help him heal quicker.

I love driving Rah's car. I can't wait to get off and get back behind the wheel. It's nothing like my ride. When I arrived at the shop this morning, the usual suspects were here plus some, and I've been working my ass off all day. I don't see how Netta ever did this alone. I look down at my ringing cell and see Rah's name pop up on the screen. Mama's waiting for me to bring her some more plastic bottles but I have to take this call.

"She's gone, Jayd, and she took Rahima with her." I drop the empty plastic containers in my hand. This isn't supposed to be happening.

"What? How did she get out of town? She doesn't have a car."

"She must've made a copy of the key and came to get my grandfather's Regal with one of her homies or something, Jayd. I don't know, but what I do know is she's turned off her cell and her grandparents don't know where she is. I knew something like this was going to happen." Everyone in the shop can hear Rah yelling through the phone, including Mama, who's working in the back.

"I'm sorry, baby. I don't know what to say."

"You should've never gave her the keys," he says, hanging up. Mama notices my face and comes out from the back to hug me, but I'm not in the mood.

"What's the use of having dreams if I can't do anything to change them?" I'm starting to really hate my powers.

"You have to have more faith in yourself, Jayd. God doesn't make mistakes, and your ancestors toiled long and hard for our lineage. Don't disrespect it by disrespecting your gifts. Your mother made that mistake and her gift became her torture. Learn form her mistake, Jayd. Seize your blessing."

"It's not a blessing—this is a curse," I say, throwing down the keys to Rah's car, tears falling down my cheeks. How could we lose Rahima in the blink of an eye?

"*Did you just say 'we'?*" my mom asks, invading my mind while Mama's still on my case. Can a sistah catch a break?

"Like I said, learn from your mother's mistakes, Jayd. All of them."

"I can't help loving Rah's daughter." I hate it when I whine.

"No, but you can help the way the situation has turned out. Didn't you have a dream about this already?" I recall the night I dreamt of myself falling because I didn't make a clear decision about how to deal with Rah, Jeremy, and Rahima. "It was a premonition that came to serve a purpose. But, as usual, you let your dreams fly by you like you don't know better. The time has come for you to catch the shit before it hits the fan and the only way you can do that is by trusting in your gift of sight completely, chile. Otherwise you're destined to keep moving like you're sleepwalking and that's dangerous in more ways than one."

"But Mama, I didn't see all of this drama coming at once." She looks at me and grits her teeth like she used to do when I'd whine as a child. She has no tolerance for whining or lying, and I think she considers me as doing both right now.

"Did I or did I not tell you about my dream of violence

and bloodshed? Did you not have a dream about damn-near the same thing? And did we not share a vision together where violence and loss played a significant role? What the hell do you think all of that was, Jayd? We don't get the luxury of dreaming casual dreams." I look down at my toes and try to hold back my tears but it's no use. Whenever Mama's this mad at me I can't help but let it flow.

"I know, Mama, and I'm sorry, but what could I do?" Mama sternly lifts my chin. She stares at me so intently I can't keep focused on my wet toes much longer. I look up into her bloodshot emerald eyes and get momentarily lost in them.

"You have to be thankful for your powers, Jayd. They're yours to keep whether you like it or not. Maybe if you had to walk in my and Maman's shoes, you'd be a little more grateful for your gift of sight. You can make all of the potions and brownies you want to, but until you respect the real power behind your dreams, all of your support materials—which is exactly what the recipes are—won't do you much good."

"But my dream didn't come true. We won the court case without having to go to trial and we still lost Rahima. How am I supposed to foresee that?" Mama lets go of my chin and gets back to work.

"Because you know Sandy's unpredictable at best." I know she wants to say crazy but she's trying to be nice. "Your dream didn't say anything about him losing in court, which he didn't. You have to pay close attention to the warnings present, and respond accordingly. Think outside of the box when helping clients and yourself, Jayd."

Mama's right. I've been too busy caring about everyone's feelings to do my job effectively.

After I get off work, I leave Rah's car at Netta's and drive my raggedy car two miles from the shop to my daddy's house and decide to park it in his driveway. He can figure out what to do with this piece of crap. I'm done being weighed down by this mess. I only keep what I want to, not what someone thinks I should have. I get out of the car, remove the few things I have in it and leave the keys in the ignition. Maybe I'll get lucky and someone will steal it. At least then I'll get some of my money back.

I carefully close the door so as not to draw any attention to myself. I know at this time of evening my daddy and step-mom are in the back watching television or asleep on their matching his-and-hers couches. I want to get out of here without confrontation. Luckily he lives two houses from the corner and the bus stops only a block after that. If I have to take the bus from now on, so be it. I'd rather keep it moving like that than be dependant on an undependable ride and man.

"I'm proud of you, girl," my mom says, making my personal moment not so private. *"By the way, Karl said I can roll the Camry and you can roll my ride indefinitely. So, you're not alone. The car is yours to keep for as long as you need it, baby."*

"For real, Mom?" I think back. I take a seat at the bus stop, watching the cars go by and pray that she's not playing with me.

"Yes, girl. Would I play with you about something as serious as this? He sees how hard you're hustling and wants to help and it just so happens he can. You can say thank you when you see him next weekend. Bye, baby, and be safe getting back."

When I finally make my way back to my mom's house in Rah's car, it's late and I'm tired to the bone. I have clients around the neighborhood all day tomorrow and I still have to get ready for school next week. It's the start of a new semester but I have a feeling it's going to be the same old drama. With Nigel and Mickey both out of my day-to-day life and Nellie sucking Chance even deeper into her fake world, I don't know who I'm going to hang with. Jeremy's proven yet again to be unsympathetic toward the tales from my hood, and I don't know if I want to hang around him like that right now. Maggie and her crew are the only ones who seem to understand me fully, and that resonates with how I'm feeling right now.

Making my way into the dark apartment, I trip over my own shit blocking the door. When I left this morning I was in such a hurry that I left my weekend bag, as well as other things, laid out on the floor. Lucky for me my mom's spending more and more time at Karl's, which leaves me to be a slob on the weekends if I so choose.

"I need to get organized," I say aloud to myself. My backpack is filled with old letters, miscellaneous papers, and other things that have no place in my life anymore. I separate the important stuff from the trash and throw the trash away. My letters go in my letter box, which I keep in the bottom of my mom's living room closet.

When I open the plain wooden box that I made in shop class in junior high, the first thing that pops out of the overstuffed thing is a letter from Rah. It's so old and has been read and reread so many times it's falling apart.

Dear Jayd,

I know I messed up big time, but I want to make it up to you. Please forgive me, girl. You know I never meant to hurt you. That's why I didn't tell you about me and Sandy or about our daughter. If I could go back in time and change everything, I would.

But I can't and I also can't live without you. Please talk to me. I love you, Rah.

I never got over the pain he caused me when he betrayed my trust. I know he feels now that in his mind I've done the same thing, but I couldn't prevent Sandy from taking off with Rahima. I hope he understands the limitations of my powers one day. I hope I understand them, too. Until then, I have to work with what I've got and hope for the best. Tonight is all about resting and trying to shake off this week. Everything else will have to wait until I wake up.

Epilogue

After braiding hair all day and pressing Shawntrese's hair, I'm tired out of my mind. Rah texted me and told me to leave his car at my mom's and he'll get it when he can. I drove my mom's car home for the first time and almost broke my neck trying to shift her clutch. I know the basics of driving a stick, but it's going to take time to get used to it. I even had to put away my iPod so that I could focus better. I'm sticking to driving the streets until I get the hang of it. I already called Mama and told her I was coming home by myself. I also told her I needed to talk about all that's happened and she's waiting with open arms. I hope those arms come with a plate of food because a sistah's starving. I haven't had a chance to eat all day and could use some of her home cooking to make me feel better.

When I get home, Mama's out back working and not in the kitchen cooking, which is where I had hoped to find her. I guess it's another burger-and-fries type of night for me. I should've stopped somewhere on my way home, but maybe I can go out and get something after I talk to Mama.

"Tragedy happens, loss happens, and death happens. That is what this odu states," Mama says, reclaiming the small cowrie shells spread out on the mat before giving them another throw. How Mama keeps all of the odu—or spiritual stories—in her head still amazes me. But she does, and insists on giving me another reading.

"So, there's nothing I can do?"

Mama breathes deeply and looks up at me before throwing the shells again. "You have to use your gift of sight to see the unseen. For you that means learning how to control your dreams and read them properly. Without cultivating your gifts you won't get very far," she says, putting the shells back in their box and rising from the mat. Mama was in the middle of her Sunday gardening and personal time in the spirit room when I got home. I feel honored she stopped her work to help me.

"I guess the only thing we can do is deal with the past and keep moving through the present. You have life so you must live," Mama says, heading back outside to till the garden. She's always careful not to damage the plants while she pulls out the weeds, a skill I have yet to acquire.

"I know, Mama. It's still hard, though, knowing I'm never going to see Tre around the block again and that my own homegirl is indirectly responsible for it." Mama looks at me and arches her eyebrow like she does when she wants to state the obvious but stops herself. I know Mickey is a little more responsible than that, but she didn't pull the trigger so I can't blame it all on her.

"You have the power to change only yourself and that means you can't change the people you associate with either. We've already talked about frenemies and other harmful people in your life. If the friends around you are doing more harm than good, it's time to let them go, and you can't feel bad about that. All growth demands shedding. Look at these squash. Now, when I first planted the seeds they had to struggle to get out of the ground. They have to deal with other plants trying to stunt their development, not because they mean to but because that's what weeds do. To move toward the sun, toward the fruition of their purpose, the weeds have to be killed, and as the plants' caretaker, that's my job."

"Are you saying I need to weed out my friends because they're not growing with me? Then I'll have no one left."

"It's like anything in life, Jayd. It's precious while it's right here in front of you. But when it's gone, you can no longer cherish the physical. Now, that doesn't mean that you forget about it or neglect the memory. But you can't let the past be your crutch. If there are issues you need to deal with in the past that are keeping you from moving forward, then deal with them." Now that's the best advice I've heard all day. I have to find a way to fix all of the mistakes I've made in the past regarding my friendships, especially with Rah. I have to figure out a way to get his daughter back and how to keep Sandy from getting away with taking Rahima again. And if controlling my dreams is the first step to doing that, I'm all for it.

Drama High, Volume 8:
KEEP IT MOVIN'

L. Divine

ABOUT THIS GUIDE

The following questions are intended to
enhance your group's reading of
DRAMA HIGH: KEEP IT MOVIN'
by L. Divine.

DISCUSSION QUESTIONS

1. If you were Jayd would you get close to Rahima? Why or why not?
2. Do you think it was fair of the school to ask Mickey to leave until after the baby's born? Would you have done the same thing as Mickey?
3. Is Misty justified in her anger toward Mickey and Jayd? Do you think she's been given a bad rap as she claims?
4. Should Nigel be asked to leave the school too? Do you think guys have it easier than girls in these situations in particular? Explain.
5. Was Jayd ungrateful to her dad about her gift? Would you have reacted the same way?
6. If you were Nellie would you still be friends with Laura after all she's done to you? Do you know of cliques like this? How do they work?
7. Write your own petition asking for what you want and don't want out of your current situation. Be honest, thoughtful, and most important, be positive.
8. Do you think Esmeralda, Misty, and Misty's mother have a genuine relationship? Do you think it's beneficial for Misty to have Esmeralda in her life as a mentor and grandmother figure? Explain.

9. Did Rah do the right thing by asking Jayd to stand up with him in front of the judge? Did he go about it right-eously, or could he have done it a little differently?

10. Was Jayd justified in her initial reaction to Rah's re-quest? What would you have done?

11. How is Jeremy's Christmas gift to Jayd different in in-tention from the other expensive gifts he's bought her in the past? Should Jayd have accepted it? Why or why not?

12. Do you think Nellie will ever go back to hanging with Jayd and her crew? If you were Jayd could you forgive Nellie?

13. Is Mickey to blame for the shooting? What steps could she have taken to keep this tragedy from occurring?

14. Should Jayd forgive Mickey for what she's done? How would you react if one of your best friends were shot?

15. Do you think Jeremy's till trying to buy Jayd's affection with expensive gifts? Do you think Jayd should accept the gifts or give them back?

16. Have you opened a bank account? Do you have a sav-ings account? Like Jayd, do most of your friends hide their money rather than put it in the bank?

17. If you were Jayd, would you have kept her car or have done what she did? Explain an alternate reaction she should've had.

Stay tuned for the next book in
the DRAMA HIGH series,
HOLIDAZE

Until then, satisfy your DRAMA HIGH craving
with the following excerpt from the next
exciting installment.

ENJOY!

Prologue

"Jayd, can you hear me?" Mama says. *But I can't see where her voice is coming from. I know I'm dreaming but it feels too real to be a dream.* "Jayd, snap out of it before you get hurt!" *Why is she tripping? All I'm doing is walking around the living room and I could walk around this entire house with my eyes closed and not trip over a thing. But wait, this isn't our living room. It looks like it but I can tell from the furniture I'm back in Maman's time, and this is her house.*

"Jon Paul, no! Give her back to me!" Maman screams at her husband, who's holding their daughter tight. The baby screams loudly as Maman's cries get even more powerful. She begins to shriek like an opera singer and my great-grandfather can't take anymore. He slaps Maman hard with the back of his hand and she falls to the floor, hitting the Christmas tree on the way down.

"Lynn Mae," Maman cries, holding her bloody face with one hand and reaching her free hand up toward her daughter, who is still in her father's arms.

"Jayd, wake up, now!" *Mama shouts but this time she's not in my dream with me. Where is her voice coming from?*

"What is she doing here?" Jon Paul asks my great-grandmother, looking dead at me. Oh hell, no. I don't want to be in this dream. Maybe I should wake up, but I can't. I have no control over when I wake up from, or fall into, my dreams.

"Yes, you do, Jayd, and now is the time to exercise that power. Wake your ass up!"

Just then, Jon Paul charges at me with his daughter in tow like he's going to slap me too. What the hell?

"Jon Paul, Sarah has nothing to do with this. Leave her alone," Maman says, now on her feet, her green eyes glowing like I've never seen before. Unlike in my last dream with Maman, this time her eyes look like emerald fireballs. He's in for it now. And who the hell is Sarah?

"She's always here. You know all about her whoreish ways, don't you, young lady?" I back away from my great-grandfather, frightened of his temper. As I stumble over a chair, I land in it and catch my reflection in a clean pot on the kitchen stove. The face staring back at me belongs to a girl about my age, but it ain't me. Ah hell, no. This is too much for me to handle.

"Jon Paul, haven't you heard of picking on someone your own size?" Maman's voice begins to get higher in pitch and her eyes are even brighter as she focuses all of her attention on him. His head begins to pulsate just like it did in the vision that Mama and I shared on Christmas Eve, and he can't take it anymore. He begins to charge toward the kitchen door, but Maman's not letting him go anywhere with her daughter.

"Aren't you forgetting something?" Maman says, putting her arms out for her daughter, whose eyes are also glowing. "Sarah, come here. And bring Lynn Mae with you. He can't hurt you now." I don't move because I don't realize she's

talking to me. But when she focuses her glowing gaze in my direction I jump up from the chair, walk toward the mentally paralyzed man and take my grandmother out of his hands. When I reach my great-grandmother, she pushes us behind her and focuses all of her energy on crippling her husband. Maman's powers are completely off the chain. And I thought Mama was gangster with her shit.

"Jayd, drink this," *Mama says, still outside of my dream. I look down at the baby in my arms and she smiles back at me, making me think of what Rahima must be doing now. But this is Mama, not Rahima, and I'm about to freak out completely if I don't wake up soon.*

"Why is Jayd standing in the middle of the living room floor so late?" *I can hear Bryan but I can't see him either. What's really going on?*

"She's sleepwalking. Help me keep her safe but don't touch her," Mama says. *Sleepwalking? Damn it. I haven't done this in years and it's never good when I do.* "Jayd, focus on my voice, not on whatever's going on in your dream and snap out of it, please!" *The urgency in Mama's voice scares me but I still can't find my way out.*

"Okay girls, it's time to make our move," *Maman says, not letting go of her visual hold on Jon Paul for a second.* "He kicked in the front door, as you can see, so we're going to have to make our way out the back. Stay behind me. And Sarah, whatever you do, don't let go of Lynn Mae." *We follow my great-grandmother back into the kitchen and walk around her husband, who is now crippled on the floor and holding his head, which looks like it's going to burst.* "Walk right by him. Don't look at him. Just keep moving and everything will be okay."

"Jayd, stop walking," *Mama says, but I can't. I have to follow Maman and get baby Mama out of harm's way.*

"Jayd, it's not real. Stop walking, now! Bryan, follow us."

I follow Maman out of the back door, hand her baby to her and she looks at me, releasing me from my dream state.

Upon waking, I fall back into Bryan's arms, completely lifeless.

"Here, Jayd. Swallow this," Mama says, forcing some thick concoction down my throat. I resist at first because the smell is putrid. Whatever's in this cup reminds me of when Mama used to make me drink orange juice mixed with castor oil when I would get constipated as a child. I still don't drink orange juice to this day because of that experience.

"Y'all are too much for a nigga sometimes, you know that?" Bryan says, holding on to me tightly as Mama continues force-feeding me. I hate it when this happens.

"Watch your mouth," Mama says to Bryan. I look up at the both of them and realize we are standing on the back porch. It's cold outside and dark. Mama's dog looks at us from her post on the bottom step and seemingly shakes her head at the sight. All Lexi does is sleep and scratch herself, so I'm really not worried about disturbing her. "Jayd, are you okay, baby?" I hear Mama but I'm feeling Bryan right now. Sometimes it's too much for me, too. If I could just leave my powers at the curb right now I'd do it in a heartbeat. I'm sick of this shit.

"I'm fine," I say, coughing up some of the thickness she's made me swallow. I'm shivering in my nightgown and sweats and my feet are bare, causing the cold to run straight through my body. "Can I go back to bed now?" If Bryan's just getting in from his radio show, it must be close to two in the morning and it's a school day for me no matter what kind of dream I just had.

"Not until you tell me what that was all about, Jayd. Whenever you sleepwalk it's serious, girl, and you know it."

"Mama, I start a new semester tomorrow and I have to drive my mom's stick shift all the way to Redondo Beach for the first time. I need sleep. Please, can we talk tomorrow?" Mama looks into my eyes and feels my pain.

"Fine, but don't forget any of it. I need details." I'm sure she's already got the summary in her mind. And I wish I could forget, but this dream was too freaky. I've never dreamt of being someone else before. I hope that was the last time it happens. I have enough to deal with as it is. I just want to get through this day with as little trouble as possible. With new classes, Mickey and Nellie tripping, and Nigel still out because of his wounded arm, there's going to be enough drama to deal with as it is.

~ 1 ~
Walk On By

"That's all that I have left, so let me hide/
The pain and the hurt that you gave me when you said goodbye."

—DIONNE WARWICK

After this morning's sleepwalking episode, I could barely get myself out of the bed, let alone dressed and ready to go. Luckily I don't have to get up as early as I did before my mom let me take her car, but six is still early in my book. Speaking of books, I forgot my backpack, rushing out the door this morning, so my day's not going to be easy, especially since we receive our new books for the semester and take them home to cover.

I'm not excited about my new class schedule because not much has really changed. That's one of the major problems with being on the Advanced Placement track: the monotony is grueling and there's always the added curse of having to deal with Mrs. Bennett. With any luck, I won't run into her or Misty today. That would make everything better.

"Damn it," I say aloud while attempting to shift the car into first gear on the steep hill near campus. There aren't many hills between Compton and Inglewood, so I never got to practice balancing the clutch in various situations. Where's Rah when I need him? He hasn't talked to me since Sandy took off in his grandfather's car with Rahima. I know he's pissed but it really wasn't my fault. How was I supposed to know she would make a copy of his keys and jack Rah the first chance she got?

"Because the bitch is crazy," my mom says, feeling my frustration.

"Mom, you can't call her a bitch. She's young enough to be your daughter," I think back, while still trying to work my way up the hill without rolling back too far. The cars behind me are honking at my slow progression but I don't care. I'd rather them be mad at me than hit anyone. All I need is to have an accident. My mom would never let me live that down.

"You worry too much, Jayd. And no, Sandy isn't old enough to be a child of mine. That girl's eighteen and a mother, therefore she's fair game and a bitch is a bitch, as I'm sure you know." My mom's got a point there. If there's an official club, Sandy's got to be the president.

"Can you help me drive this thing or what?" I say aloud. If the traffic weren't so slow trying to get into the parking lot I wouldn't have this problem. I've experienced more stop-and-go in the ten minutes I've been waiting in line here than my mother does on the 405 freeway during rush hour.

"You have to learn how to drive in all situations, Jayd. Besides, it's good for you to know how to drive a stick. It's an irreplaceable skill to have. Now, the first thing you need to do is calm down, little one, and put the car in neutral." I follow my mom's instructions and the car starts to slide backwards. *"Put your foot on the brake, Jayd! Damn, girl, you have to use your common sense always."*

"Mom, I had a very rough night. Please cut me some slack," I say, near tears. I notice the new girl, Shawn, walking past me and looking at me like I'm crazy. I guess she heard that about me and probably thinks I'm talking to myself. I don't care what she thinks of me. As long as she keeps walking, it's all good.

"Okay, I'm sorry. Now, ease off of the brake and apply an equal amount of pressure on the clutch before shifting into first gear. Then, press slightly on the gas. If you do it right, the car should go smoothly up the hill." At first, the car lurches forward, but then I ease up on the clutch and press the gas simultaneously. It works smoothly, just like my mother said it would.

"Thank you, Mom," I think back.

"That's what I'm here for. Now, what about this rough night?" I pull up in line and feel like an old pro at driving a stick the way I'm handling the hill. I'm almost in a good mood for the first time in days and don't want to mess it up thinking about my dream.

"Mom, I really don't want to go into that right now." I'm next in line to get through the gate and really want to get on with my day. It's bad enough Rah still hasn't returned any of my calls or text messages since he picked up his Acura from my mother's house yesterday. I want to know if he's heard from Rahima. I know he feels like he's the only one missing his daughter, but I miss her too, and I need to know if he's heard from Rahima's crazy-ass mama.

"Okay, fine. But I will remind you this weekend when I see you. Have a good day, baby, and let me know how your day went later on."

"Alright, Mom. You too," I think back. I have to watch it talking aloud to her when I'm in public. I already have a reputation as a voodoo girl. The last thing I need is the school thinking I'm a schizoid, too.

"Hey, Jayd, new wheels again?" Jeremy says from his car to mine, catching me off guard. Somehow he's pulled way up beside me, putting his car in the perfect position to ease his way behind mine and to be next in line to get through the gate. I guess being the most popular guy on campus has its advantages even before the school day begins.

"Yeah, my mom had sympathy for me and let me roll her car until I get wheels of my own." I haven't heard from my daddy since I left my dilapidated vehicle he bought me for Christmas in his driveway Saturday night, and don't expect to hear from him anytime soon. I know he's pissed and his ego's shattered. It'll take awhile for him to come around and call me this time.

"Sweet. So when are you taking me out for a change?" I'm still irritated with Jeremy for the way he didn't react when I told him about Nigel and Tre getting shot last week, but what can I expect? His reality is surfing all day and living the life of luxury while mine is making potions with my grandmother and dodging the occasional bullet.

"One day," I say as I pull into the lot to find a spot. Jeremy's right behind me, ready to get on with this school day as well. I don't know how I'm going to stay focused, but as Mama says, the day will pass whether I participate in it or not. So we'll just have to wait and see how it goes because right now, I feel like time is passing me right on by and that's not good.

START YOUR OWN BOOK CLUB

Courtesy of the DRAMA HIGH series

ABOUT THIS GUIDE

The following is intended to help you get
the book club you've always wanted
up and running!
Enjoy!

Start Your Own Book Club

A Book Club is not only a great way to make friends, but it is also a fun and safe environment for you to express your views and opinions on everything from fashion to teen pregnancy. A Teen Book Club can also become a forum or venue to air grievances and plan remedies for problems.

The People

To start, all you need is yourself and at least one other person. There's no criteria for who this person or persons should be other than them having a desire to read and a commitment to discuss things during a certain time frame.

The Rules

Just as in Jayd's life, sometimes even Book Club discussions can be filled with much drama. People tend to disagree with each other, cut each other off when speaking, and take criticism personally. So, there should be some ground rules:

1. Do not attack people for their ideas or opinions.
2. When you disagree with a book club member on a point, disagree respectfully. This means that you do not denigrate other people for their ideas or even their ideas themselves, i.e., no name calling or saying, "That's stupid!" Instead, say, "I can respect your position; however, I feel differently."
3. Back up your opinions with concrete evidence, either from the book in question or life in general.
4. Allow everyone a turn to comment.
5. Do not cut a member off when the person is speaking. Respectfully wait your turn.
6. Critique only the idea. Do not criticize the person.

7. Every member must agree to and abide by the ground rules.

Feel free to add any other ground rules you think might be necessary.

The Meeting Place

Once you've decided on members, and agreed to the ground rules, you should decide on a place to meet. This could be the local library, the school library, your favorite restaurant, a bookstore, or a member's home. Remember, though, if you decide to hold your sessions at a member's home, the location should rotate to another member's home for the next session. It's also polite for guests to bring treats when attending a Book Club meeting at a member's home. If you choose to hold your meetings in a public place, always remember to ask the permission of the librarian or store manager. If you decide to hold your meetings in a local bookstore, ask the manager to post a flyer in the window announcing the Book Club to attract more members if you so desire.

Timing Is Everything

Teenagers of today are all much busier than teenagers of the past. You're probably thinking, "Between chorus rehearsals, the Drama Club, and oh yeah, my job, when will I ever have time to read another book that doesn't feature Romeo and Juliet!" Well, there's always time, if it's time well-planned and time planned ahead. You and your Book Club can decide to meet as often or as little as is appropriate for your bustling schedules. *Once a month* is a favorite option. *Sleepover Book Club* meetings—if you're open to excluding one gender—is also a favorite option. And in this day of high-tech, savvy teens, *Internet Discussion Groups* are also an appealing option. Just choose what's right for you!

Well, you've got the people, the ground rules, the place, and the time. All you need now is a book!

The Book

Choosing a book is the most fun. KEEP IT MOVIN' is of course an excellent choice, and since it's part of a series, you won't soon run out of books to read and discuss. Your Book Club can also have comparative discussions as you compare the first book, THE FIGHT, to the second, SECOND CHANCE, and so on.

But depending upon your reading appetite, you may want to veer outside of the Drama High series. That's okay. There are plenty of options, many of which you will be able to find under the Dafina Books for Young Readers Program in the coming months.

But don't be afraid to mix it up. Nonfiction is just as good as fiction and a fun way to learn about from where we came without just using a history textbook. Science fiction and fantasy can be fun, too!

And always, always research the author. You might find that the author has a Web site where you can post your Book Club's questions or comments. The author may even have an e-mail address available so you can correspond directly. Authors might also sit in on your Book Club meetings, either in person, or on the phone, and this can be a fun way to discuss the book as well!

The Discussion

Every good Book Club discussion starts with questions. KEEP IT MOVIN', as does every book in the Drama High series, comes with a Reading Group Guide for your convenience, though of course, it's fine to make up your own. Here are some sample questions to get started:

1. What's this book all about anyway?
2. Who are the characters? Do we like them? Do they remind us of real people?
3. Was the story interesting? Were real issues that are of concern to you examined?
4. Were there details that didn't quite work for you or ring true?
5. Did the author create a believable environment—one that you could visualize?
6. Was the ending satisfying?
7. Would you read another book from this author?

Record Keeper

It's generally a good idea to have someone keep track of the books you read. Often libraries and schools will hold reading drives where you're rewarded for having read a certain number of books in a certain time period. Perhaps a pizza party awaits!

Get Your Teachers and Parents Involved

Teachers and parents love it when kids get together and read. So involve your teachers and parents. Your Book Club may read a particular book whereby it would help to have an adult's perspective as part of the discussion. Teachers may also be able to include what you're doing as a Book Club in the classroom curriculum. That way, books you love to read, such as the Drama High ones, can find a place in your classroom alongside the books you don't love to read so much.

Resources

To find some new favorite writers, check out the following resources. Happy reading!

Young Adult Library Services Association
http://www.ala.org/ala/yalsa/yalsa.htm

Carnegie Library of Pittsburgh
Hip-Hop!
Teen Rap Titles
http://www.carnegielibrary.org/teens/read/booklists/teen rap.html

TeensPoint.org
What Teens Are Reading
http://www.teenspoint.org/reading_matters/book_list.asp?s ort=5&list=274

Teenreads.com
http://www.teenreads.com

Sacramento Public Library
Fantasy Reading for Kids
http://www.saclibrary.org/teens/fantasy.html

Book Divas
http://www.bookdivas.com

Meg Cabot Book Club
http://www.megcabotbookclub.com